THREADING TROUBLE

A QUILTING COZY MYSTERY

KATHRYN MYKEL

Edited by Nia Quinn & Sharp Eyed Shari
Cover Design by PixelSquirrel
Formatted by Kathryn Mykel

Special thanks to my family, friends & peers.
Props to my co-working group for showing up every morning.
To the brilliant editors who polish my work and make me look good!
And most of all a huge thank you to all of the dedicated readers, quilters, and fans!

I could not do it all without your support and encouragement.

CONTENTS

1

THEY WERE MUTTERLY MISTAKEN

THE DAY AFTER CHRISTMAS

Alex Bailey was a bundle of nerves, eager—no, *desperate*—for a change of location. Her life had been a whirl of activity leading up to her first holiday season back home on Spruce Street.

After the mutterly mistaken debacle at the local Christmas quilt show, and nursing a burnt hand during the reopening celebration of the quilt shop, Nuts & Bolts.

Nineteen hours in a luxury SUV, through the blizzard, with a gassy dog and her sister-from-another-mister—no problem!

Approaching the 'Welcome to Mishap, Georgia' sign, Alex let out a nervous laugh and inhaled a big gulp of air, only to be assaulted by the noxious scent of her canine companion's flatulence. "Gross." Alex pushed the 'window down' button repeatedly with her finger, and the window went haywire, along with her already fried nerves.

Drive. It'll be fun, they said.

Alex's gag reflex set in, Charlotte stared at her with a bewildered expression. "What's happening to you over there? Do we need to pull over? Are you going to make it, we're almost there."

"I'm fine, it's Kibbles! Can't you smell that?"

Charlotte chuckled. "Smells 'earthy' to me. What have you been feeding her? Never mind. The fact that you give her carrots for a 'treat' tells me all I need to know." Charlotte ruffled the dog's wiry fur in all directions so the pup looked like Alex felt.

This is going to be so much more fun than a holiday quilt show with missing quilts, a doped-up dog and a misguided mayor!

Kibbles, the dog named after dog food by her homicidal previous owner, didn't bat an eyelash at the attention—blissfully unaware of her human's discomfort as she slept, dead to the world. Alex stared at her canine companion inquisitively. *Do dogs have eyelashes? They must.*

Alex let out a contented breath. Truth be told, Alex was indeed grateful for the change of pace that came from the two day driving adventure from Massachusetts to Georgia.

"Don't worry, Kibby, Auntie Char will feed you the *good stuff* this week."

"You know, you are starting to sound a bit like me. Baby talk and slang are telltale signs of new dog ownership."

Charlotte ignored Alex's quip by turning her head, but the crack of a smile gave away her good humor about the situation.

Despite the nail-biting, white-knuckling, and breath-holding, Alex and Charlotte finally arrived in Mishap, Georgia . . . without mishap—and Alex pulled up to the curb and idled.

"Are you sure it makes sense to have brought the dog in the first place?" her best friend, Charlotte, asked, her voice now muffled by her hand covering her mouth and nose. "Pew! Okay, that one curled my nose hairs."

Alex pulled forward, holding her breath, and turned into the parking lot across from their final destination—#6 Society Square. A massive stone theater, the *Eureka Theater Company,* loomed over the square, casting an ominous shadow that blocked out the late day sun. Alex leaned forward to peer out the window at the castle-like facade. An event banner hung from a wrought iron balcony, flapping against a relentless wind. It read:

Gretta Galia Memorial Theater

All was quiet inside the SUV as they gaped at the property, save for the snoring dog, the buzz of the electric engine, and the light hum of hot air flowing through the heating vents.

Sitting back against her seat, Alex finally replied to Charlotte's question. "When I spoke to Liam, he insisted I bring the dog. He must be an animal lover."

"How did he even know you have a dog?" Charlotte asked, stroking the tiny black-and-tan mutt in her lap.

"From when we went on the cruise and Alastor watched the dog for me. Watched being a loose description."

"I really hope this Liam guy isn't a curmudgeon like his brother." Charlotte blew out a deep breath, which fogged the passenger window beside her face. She drew a stick figure in the condensation with her index finger.

"I really hope I'm not going to own yet another of Nona's lavish gifts!" Alex sighed.

"Did Nona buy this theater?" Charlotte's voice was shrill.

Alex shrugged, "I had a sneaking suspicion of just that, when I opened the invitation for this event."

Kibbles replied with an affirmative single bark. "Woof."

"I don't think we came all the way to Mishap, Georgia for a theater building dedication—in Nona's name—for anything less than a transfer of property," Alex replied sarcastically. "I'm betting she *did*."

"Someone's going to have to explain to me how she managed all this behind our backs." Charlotte sighed.

"More like how she managed this right under our noses." A pang of guilt over Nona's death made Alex's stomach drop.

All I want is to put the past year behind me and get on with a new stage of my life.

Kibbles stirred. Alex's studied the dog and her heart swelled.

What exactly is *this new chapter?*

She'd left her career less than a year ago, and returned home to Spruce Street to help Nona, then had to step into the role of matriarch after her death. Alex was learning to expect the unexpected.

So, what's next? Retiring to a newly gained island, or taking charge of a theater company?

Each scenario was more ludicrous than the last as she gave credence to how her life had devolved since she'd left New York. Only one person made the chaos worth it—*Hawk.*

I should've brought him too.

Upon receiving the invitation to the glum sight before them, Alex had immediately wanted to bring Hawk—a private investigator who'd stuck by her through all the drama and danger. But her gut had told her this trip would be *all about Nona*, and bringing Charlotte—Nona's biological granddaughter—was the more sensible decision.

There will be plenty of time to spend with Hawk when we head off to Madras.

Her daydream immediately drifted to the island. She was there in spirit already, the warm sun on her face, the silky sand between her toes . . . and the fun coeds she'd met on the *quilting calamity* cruise.

Though they were amazingly self-sufficient, she couldn't ignore that they were her responsibility now.

Hawk's there taking care of everything.

She wiggled her toes in the beach sand of her daydream and then pulled her phone out of her messenger bag and sent a quick text.

ALEX:

Hope you're enjoying the sun!

It's almost as cold here as it is in Salem.

Her quiet return to Spruce Street and the life she lived before her career, felt like one of those lame jokes that because she'd heard it a million times—had no energy, surprise, or humor. Just as bad as a quilting guild without its leader; a neighborhood mourning their matriarch; a dilapidated marine biology school full of students, on a remote island; and now a gloom-and-doom theater.

A gloom-and-doom theater? Complete with what? An acting troupe? What else *am I going to find here? How many more people am I going to be in charge of?*

Her only hope now was Nona hadn't spent their shared money on this property also. Though she wouldn't deny this mystery was a slight reprieve from the last conundrum she'd found herself amidst—the bones of her former boss's sister, surfacing in a plot of undeveloped land Nona had purchased a dozen years ago.

Alex's breathing quickened at each of her passing thoughts. She sat in the car, staring blindly through the haze created by the fog and ice crystals that had crept up the windshield.

I couldn't make this stuff up if I tried! What on earth am I going to do with a theater company?

Charlotte interrupted Alex's runaway thought train, "Does his brother, Alastor, know about all this?"

Alex paused and considered her answer. "No. Liam was clear that *this* matter, at least, is just between us." She motioned to Charlotte and the air in and around the triangle of three people, one of whom was Liam, who they had not yet met.

"I hope we're not staying in that creepy old house." Charlotte wiped the windshield with her palm and peeked out.

Across the square from the theater stood, in serious disrepair, a two story mansion with gothic architecture.

"Well, unless the *theater* has bedrooms, my guess is that's Liam's house," Alex quipped.

"Is it weird that the man who is supposedly the 'key' lives in a haunted mansion and the curmudgeon on our block lives in a cute little gingerbread house?"

Alex laughed so hard she snorted. "Hmm. That's funny."

"Maybe not *that* funny?"

Alex fished for a hankie in her purse. After finding one, she blew her nose.

Charlotte stared off into space. "I hope he's not a hoarder." Her expression changed from dismay to disdain.

"I hope the place isn't really haunted." Alex shivered.

Kibbles agreed, "Woof."

Alex flicked the defrost button and cranked the heat to full blast. She held her hands out to the air vent, which was blasting hot air every which way. An errant hair flew into her eye and she tucked it haphazardly into her messy bun.

The condensation cleared from the windshield enough to reveal a shadow. Alex wiped a wider circle, which revealed a lanky elderly man standing inches from the front of her BMW. She looked down to make sure the car was in park and then cut the engine.

"That's not creepy at all," Charlotte muttered, and Kibbles jumped to all fours, her hackles raised, though she remained quiet.

"He looks . . . harmless . . . enough . . . He can't be more than a hundred and twenty pounds." Alex laughed. "Of all the villains we've encountered lately, I doubt *he's* one."

"I thought he was supposed to be a good guy?" Charlotte asked.

"Yes, I'm sure he is. You said he was—never mind. Let's get

on with it." Alex sighed, and Kibbles jumped into her lap. "At least let me get my seat belt off first, Kibbles."

Kibbles climbed up onto Alex's shoulder.

"I think that dog is more like a cat than a dog." Charlotte grinned. "Or a bird, the way she's perched." Charlotte plucked the dog off Alex's shoulder just before Alex's seat belt clicked open.

Alex palmed the car keys. "You hold her, and I'll grab the bags. I'll get the crate later once, we're settled."

Kibbles whined, and Charlotte scratched the pup's head, cooing, "Give her a break, you mama's dog!"

The two women stepped out of the vehicle, and a blast of wind hit Alex like a slap in the face. She grimaced, clutching her purse—her hand inside it, holding on to her mace.

Just in case.

She had to be on guard after multiple attempts on her life. The so-called *adventures* Nona had been sending her on were proving more and more dangerous each time. From a hit woman implanted on her street, to a murderous couple on the cruise, she hadn't the faintest notion what she was in for *here*, or if she'd be *safe*.

2

LIKE A BATCAVE

MISHAP, GEORGIA

Out in the chill of the unseasonably frigid winter's day, Alex snuggled deeper into her heavy coat, adjusting her fur-lined hood to block out the biting cold. She glanced around at the unfamiliar landscape, taking in the sight of barren trees around the courtyard.

"Hi, you must be Liam," Alex exclaimed in a strained voice to the man before them, dressed in a worn-out black suit, complemented with a faded bow tie.

Add penguin tails, and he'll be the butler.

Liam stepped closer and held out his hand when he was in arm's reach of Alex. The most genuine smile crossed his face, and a warmth radiated from his toffee-brown eyes.

"Yes. Welcome to Mishap, Alex."

Alex sighed with relief and unclenched her hand from the mace canister in her purse, raising her hand to meet his. His skin was cold against hers, his handshake firm.

He turned toward the others. "Charlotte. Kibbles," he greeted them, and waved. "Come. Let's get you settled in after your long journey."

Kibbles flashed a hairy eyeball at the man. Alex stifled a grin but caught the dubious look Charlotte flashed him as well.

Alex popped the trunk open and grabbed their travel bags and Kibbles's backpack.

I swear this dog has more stuff *than I do now.*

Alex followed behind Charlotte, who followed Liam. Charlotte stopped and let Kibbles down to do her business in the square between the theater building and the haunted house. Kibbles lifted her leg on a stone statue or some sort covered with a blue tarp.

Liam stopped and waited for the trio with his hands tucked into his suit-jacket pockets.

The small pup scouted the perfect spot—her tail hooked upward.

Fishing a poop bag out of the back pocket of her skinny jeans, Charlotte grumbled, "Auntie will get this one."

The wind howled, threatening to drown out her words.

"It's just as cold here as it is in Mass," Alex said, and rubbed her hands together.

"Let's get inside, I have a fire burning. Much more pleasant than this unseasonable weather we're having." Liam ushered them toward the front of the house. "It's usually in the mid-fifties this time of year, not thirties."

The sun cast an ominous orange glow behind the house, creating a ghostly atmosphere. Alex glowered at the house suspiciously. She stared up the rickety steps of the foreboding building. A once grand entrance was now in disrepair, with broken floorboards, chipped paint and cracked windowpanes. Alex spotted a modern security camera, not so conspicuously hidden in one of the eves of the porch roof.

Alex entered the dwelling behind Charlotte and was instantly warmed by the toasty ambience. Despite the signs of neglect on the exterior, the inside was well kept and opened to a grand room full of oversized plush furnishings.

"This place is so cozy," Charlotte commented, running her hand along a velvety armrest. A chandelier sparkled with the glow of candlelight. Alex swirled around, taking in her surroundings, and the golden floor planks creaked with each step she took, but the sound only added to the charm. The house was immaculate despite a faint musty smell.

Liam blinked, glancing toward a woman standing in the doorway. "Oh, here's my assistant, Emmie." He smiled at a rotund, older woman in overalls, and Emmie extended her hand while walking toward Alex.

"Hi, nice to meet you both," she said, and shifted to shake hands with Charlotte.

Liam continued, "Emmie acts as an assistant to me, as well as performing an important role in the play." He excitedly clapped his hands and turned to Alex and Charlotte, "This is great! Introductions have been made, so let's get you two settled, now. I've prepared two rooms for you upstairs." Liam waved his hand toward the grand staircase. "Just at the top, there. I'll give you some time. Come back down when you're ready."

Charlotte started up the steps and then paused. "Ready for what?"

"The tour, of course." Liam flashed a genuine smile.

"Or food?" Charlotte asked.

Liam bowed his head. "Of course, we'll have something ready for you." He nodded to Emmie then headed down the hall, and the two of them disappeared behind a set of swinging doors.

"Charlotte," Alex scolded.

"Whaaat? I'm starving!"

After grabbing the travel crate for Kibbles and then settling into her room, which was reminiscent of a lavish bed-and-breakfast—complete with a four-poster bed—she joined the others downstairs to stuff herself from a charcuterie board fit for a party.

Alex stifled a yawn.

With Kibbles tucked into her arms for her own comfort as much as the dog's, she begrudgingly followed Liam on his guided tour.

Charlotte bounced along in front of Alex.

How is Charlotte as fresh as a Georgia peach?

The walls of the home were a warm, buttery yellow, and rocking chairs, covered in floral quilts and pillows, were nestled into corners of the spacious rooms. Portraits decorated the walls, and intricately carved moldings added a touch of opulence. The whole place was a contradiction of style.

Just like Nona. Decorated with all her favorite things.

"Right this way, ladies." Liam ushered the pair of friends into a library. The tiny pup, who was back on the floor now, ran to keep up with the humans, her nails tip-tapping on the hardwood floor. The over-sized room was magnificently decorated with towering shelves that reached to the high ceiling. The shelves—filled with books of all shapes and sizes—begged to be explored. The scent of musty paper and old leather pervaded the air, creating a sense of mystery and intrigue.

Shock crossed Charlotte's face, and Alex leered at the portrait Charlotte was staring at.

"Nona?" Alex uttered. "But . . ."

"She was the queen of her castle. Even here," Liam replied with a slight grin.

Charlotte burst into laughter, stepping closer to the portrait of Nona dressed like Queen Elizabeth, complete with a hat and pearls.

"I don't know what to make of this place, Liam. Truth be told, we thought you two were—" Alex shot a look at Charlotte.

"Lovers," Charlotte said bluntly.

Liam blushed, and he tucked his hands back into his pockets. "Oh no, we weren't romantically acquainted. We shared a great affection for each other, yes. Given more time, maybe—" He stopped, turned toward the wall of books, and pulled out a tome. The tall bookshelf pivoted open, revealing a hidden passage and set of steps.

"Are you like a butler?" Charlotte asked. Pointing to the opening in the wall, she added, "Is this like Batman's lair?"

"I guess you could look at it that way," Liam replied innocently.

"But what is all this?" Alex's eyes zeroed in on the symbol on the wall of the stairwell. She stepped forward and touched the carving, Kibbles whining at her feet. "This symbol. What does it mean, Liam? We found it in the statues and on the keys—"

Charlotte peered past both of them, as she asked, "Do you know about the statues, Liam?"

"Yes of course. How do you think Nona managed to send her likeness from the grave?" He grinned.

"Did you commission the statue of Nona and ship it to Spruce Street?" Alex asked.

Failing to answer her most recent question Liam answered Alex's previous one instead. "The symbol is for the Society of Six, a secret society founded about sixty years ago. I don't know the true origins of the group, but one of the first members came from the United Kingdom."

"A secret society? For what purpose? And how was Nona involved? And how far down do those stairs go?" Charlotte bombarded Liam with questions and pointed to the stairway just beyond where they were standing.

"You've got lots of questions, I understand. We have time, I promise. Before you leave, you will have the answers you seek. Well, the answers I have knowledge of, at least." Liam gave Charlotte a reassuring smile like that of a grandfather. It was hard to be discontent with his reply.

He's adorable.

Alex observed the elderly man curiously as he ushered them down the steps. She picked up Kibbles and tucked the pooch under her arm.

The stairs led down to a cavernous room, and Alex envisioned Alice being transported to a wonderland for the likes of Cage, Connery or Cruise.

The setting sun, visible outside the solitary window, cast a dim glow into the room. The walls, adorned with vintage lamps, maps and artifacts, hinted at a hidden knowledge and power contained within the chilly grotto. Alex immediately walked toward a large armchair centered in the space. She brushed her hand over the soft, worn leather. *Have I time-warped into a scene from a classic detective novel or spy movie?*

Ancient spyglasses were poised on wooden and stone pedestals—a curious mix with newer, modern technology. Alex reached out and fiddled with a contraption perched on a plinth —a cylindrical brass tube with spinning letters and numbers.

Some type of decoder?

Liam gently removed it from her hands and replaced it on its velvet-covered perch.

"I should probably dispense the most pertinent information

first. That will give you time to digest the details over the course of your stay here." Liam spoke in a measured tone.

"Sounds like he's about to tell you that you own a dramatic arts facility, Alex," Charlotte said, and laughed, her blonde beach curls flinging around. Alex knew her sister-friend all too well—Charlotte was laughing *at* her and not *with* her, besides, Alex wasn't laughing!

"Well, yes, Charlotte, that's correct. The *Eureka Theater Company*. Soon to be the *Gretta Galia Memorial Theater*." Liam turned to Alex, addressing her. "This is, in fact, all yours." With a serious face he added, "Surprise."

Alex groaned.

Ignoring her protest, Liam continued, "Nona purchased the two buildings—this home and the theater next door—some time ago in an auction of the property. She's a local hero, you know."

"I bet," Charlotte replied, tracing her finger around a hammered golden ring, the size of a dessert plate, balanced on a metal stand.

Alex picked up a familiar silver case, a twin to the one found on Spruce Street. She recalled the conversation she'd had with Doc just over a month ago, about a list of names they'd found in a cigarette case just like the one she now held in her hand—with what she had just learned was the Society of Six symbol engraved on it.

Rebecca Briggs—whereabouts unknown. Gretta Galia—deceased. Fiona Bailey, her mom—deceased. Alexandra Bailey—safe. For now.

Liam continued, though Alex was deep in her memory of the past events. "She saved the two buildings from ruin and the charming town of Mishap from being overrun by big box developers." He turned to Charlotte. "She paid pennies on the dollar—very savvy, your grandmother."

"How does this all add up?" Alex asked.

"It's how we kept you safe. By keeping the Society alive, but secret. Even from you."

Charlotte scanned a vintage map with a curious eye, and asked, "Who else knows?"

"Precious few, to be sure. This job I do, here, Alex, it used to be your father's, rest his soul." Liam crossed himself. "After his unfortunate demise, someone needed to look after the *Batcave,* as you liken it."

"My father? What about the others?" Alex grimaced. Sadness punched her in the gut at the thought of her deceased parents. All she wanted was the resolution of the endless enigmas in her life.

Before Liam could answer Alex's questions, Charlotte asked, "Is that why *you* are the key, Liam?"

"Yes. Metaphorically and figuratively. . . and actually," he answered. "Did you bring the keys?"

"Yes." Alex fished the three keys out of her back pocket.

"Excellent, we'll get to those later." He covered her hand, closing her fingers around the keys. Turning away from Alex, Liam flittered over to a vintage phonograph set in a carved wooden cabinet. Within seconds Liam had it wound up, and the large horn was amplifying a harmonious tune that filled the space. Alex breathed in the earthy aroma of the room, and her shoulders dropped as she exhaled.

"There," Liam said, with a contented smile, as he turned back toward the women. Changing the subject, he continued, "Let me tell you a bit about the institution. We've slowly been developing the property. Once we got our accreditations back, we began working on the interior and exterior updates to the theater building. Little by little over the last few years."

Alex pushed the keys back into her jeans pocket.

Liam frowned and folded his hands behind his back, "It pains me that Nona won't see her work come to fruition."

Alex picked up a small Crumb quilt sample that had been cobbled together out of thousands of vintage and new fabrics alike.

Liam nodded. "She certainly was thrifty, your grandmother."

Alex immediately felt Charlotte's stare on her back. Nona was Charlotte's grandmother by blood, but she was no less Alex's, by choice.

Liam frowned, but his eyes gave away his affection for Nona. He took Alex's arm and led her back toward the stairwell. Stopping at the base of the steps, he pointed out the window. "It's beautiful, isn't it?"

Spotlights shone on the front facade of the theater building, and from their vantage point Alex had a perfect line of sight to the larger-than-life sign at street level—*Gretta Galia Memorial Theater*. But what Liam was pointing to was the building itself. "Nona had the foresight to know this was a diamond in the rough. And a much-needed home base for the Society."

"What the *H E* double hockey sticks are *you* going to do with a theater, Alex? In Mishap, Georgia?" Charlotte balked.

"Well, I'm not *moving here*, that's for sure. I've got an island calling my name."

Liam remained austere.

"I have my heart set on retiring to said island, which I now own—also thanks to Nona—not to a city in the middle of Georgia. No offense."

She gave him a pleading look. This man's features were nothing like those of her Spruce Street neighbor, the local curmudgeon, Alastor—nor was Liam behaving in any paranoid way like his old trout of a brother always does.

She adjusted Kibbles, who was restless under her arm.

"Oh, I understand completely. I can maintain these properties, I assure you. There's no need for you to stress over it."

Alex blew out a deep breath, that neither helped her digest the fact she was destined to be part of a generations-old secret society, nor dispelled the sick feeling in her stomach that the life she'd known wasn't really the life she'd thought it was.

"Where are the students?" Charlotte asked. "Are they even called students?"

"Well, yes, they are students *of the arts*, but they are all grown adults. Of varying ages, I might add. They're busy getting ready for the show. Burning the midnight oil, as they say." A wide smile showed his yellowing teeth. "We have a sold-out show the day before New Year's Eve. With the unveiling of the dedication—and now having you, the new benefactor, in town—it's going to be quite a spectacle."

"Spectacle? I'm not making any speeches," Alex huffed.

"No, no. Maybe just a little shine of the spotlight and a wave. Can you do that? The crowd will eat it up."

"Or eat *me* up," Alex mumbled.

3

NO ONE HERE KNOWS HOW TO MEND?

Kibbles whined and wriggled in Alex's arms again.

"Kibbles needs a potty break, and I could use some fresh air." It wasn't like the dog to fuss so much. While scratching the dog's head, Alex shushed her, murmuring, "Settle down, you wittle mutt."

"Oh, she's not a mutt," Liam spoke confidently, and Alex stopped in her tracks. "She comes from a long line of well-trained animals. The Society used to train corgis, until they arrived in America and realized the potential of hiding unassuming dogs, and cats, in plain sight."

Kibbles barked twice and covered her eye with her paw.

"You might say she's royalty, as far as the Society is concerned," Liam added.

Kibbles let out an approving "woof" before turning up her nose.

"Did she just snub her nose at us?" Charlotte asked.

"I think so," Alex replied with a chuckle, and rubbed Kibbles's head, matting her fur up. "Let's get her royal highness out to the courtyard before we have a royal accident."

Kibbles scurried around looking for a patch to do her business, while the humans admired the craftsmanship of the intricate stonework on the exterior of the theater. Once they headed inside, the trio was greeted immediately upon stepping inside the theater by a twentysomething in an electric-blue romper. Her curly red hair was piled atop her head in a giant ball.

Alex put her hand to her own long, wavy hair. *Hers must be even longer than mine.*

"Professor Arnold, will you stitch these?" She handed a pair of sequined pants to Liam.

He held them up. "Suzie, where's Roy? Can't we get him to hem these for you?" To Alex, he explained, "Roy's our current seamster. He does buttons and zippers too." Liam looked around the bustling backstage area. "Quite handy to have around, that guy."

"I can't find Roy," Suzie said.

Liam glanced at Alex, and then his eyes darted to Charlotte.

Charlotte threw her hands up. "Hey, don't look at us, we're *quilters*, not tailors."

Liam handed the britches toward Alex, and she shook her head and backed up a step. "Not me! Like she said, *quilters*!" Alex pointed between herself and Charlotte.

"Isn't it the same thing?" Liam asked, his expression confused.

"No," both Alex and Charlotte bellowed in unison.

"I'll take those, Professor." Emmie stood there with a clipboard in one hand and snatched the pants from Liam. "No need to find Roy . . . or bother the professor, Suzie. I'll handle this."

"Ladies, this is Suzie—" His smile brightened. "Suzie is a marvel on the stage. She plays the perfect feline."

Suzie blushed. "Thanks, Professor."

Emmie grunted and moved to step away.

Liam held out a hand. "Thank you, Emmie, but you've enough to do. Best go find Roy to handle that."

Suzie grimaced. "The thing is, Professor, no one's seen Roy since breakfast."

"Well, he's probably run off through the—" Emmie started.

Charlotte interrupted, "Surely someone else here must know how to sew, Liam? This is a theater company, after all. Don't you make all your costumes?"

"Don't fuss, dear. Emmie will take care of the matter if Roy can't. But to answer your question, since Nona passed, we've been looking for a new seamstress or sewing instructor, to no avail. The young adults today don't come with the home economic skills *we* were taught in our time." His eyes were bright and sincere. "I'll show you the quilting studio."

Charlotte looked at the seventy-year-old, butler-ish man. "*Our* time?" But then a smile crept across her face. "Quilting studio?"

"We had a full-time costume maker, however, she left without notice. Such a shame. Roy has done a great job filling in, but I'm afraid he's not very good." He continued leading them through a dimly lit hallway.

"I don't know who he's calling 'we,'" Charlotte whispered to Alex. "He's nearly twice our age. And why didn't he tell us there was a quilting studio sooner?"

Alex half-heartedly smiled and shrugged in reply to Charlotte.

They stopped to admire the soundboard, which looked like a computer from a bad eighties movie. Charlotte yawned and rolled her eyes.

"Ladies, this is Harrison, and that there is Dave."

"Hi." The men looked up and acknowledged the pair of spectators and their dog.

Liam whispered, "No one knows exactly what Harrison does, but he's a genius with the lighting and sound." Liam winked.

Harrison set down a small electronic box and waved, then he mocked a bow.

He's charming, that's for sure.

Liam, Alex, Charlotte and Kibbles exited the theater into the frigid evening air. Spotlights shone on the front facade of the theater building.

"As you saw, ladies, we've done all the updates to the audience-facing areas." He pointed to the entrance to the theater. "And the exterior of the theater, while an imposing relic of a structure, *has* had significant updates." The trio was walking through the courtyard between the two buildings and Liam nodded to the house. "I fear the exterior of the main home still needs quite a bit of work."

"I do see. I'm already making a list," Alex replied. "I should really feed Kibbles. Can we head back in now?"

"Meow, chirp, chirp."

"Who's this handsome fellow?" Alex bent to pat the approaching cat who was slinking around a bare potted tree, his marmalade fur a stark contrast to the winter grays all around.

Liam answered, "That's Chirp."

"Chirp, chirp, chirp."

"What say you sir? There's no danger here," Liam responded to Chirp's alarm call.

A sudden chill ran down Alex's spine and goosebumps rose on her arms. She instinctively looked over her shoulder and back at Liam, "So, none of this," Alex waved her hand around at the building that housed Liam and the secret society business, "has anything to do with the Mafia? It's just secret society business?"

"I wouldn't say *nothing* to do with the Mafia," Liam replied to Alex, gesturing for her to go up the front steps before him.

"How does this all connect with New York and Remo Romano's sister Eleanor?" Alex wondered aloud as she climbed the steps and went inside.

The legal case over the remains that had surfaced in Alex and Nona's hometown continued to loom over their good names. Nona, though deceased, was still a suspect for Eleanor's murder, because said bones had been found on Alex's property —the very property Nona had demanded Alex buy long ago. After the authorities conducted an exhaustive search of the property, they were confident no other bodies were buried there. If not for Officer Mark, and Nona's son, the mayor—both residents of Spruce Street—they likely would have hauled Alex in for the crime. The case remained open and unsolved even as Alex traveled to Mishap.

The definitive proof that the bones belonged to the sister of Alex's former employer, Remo Romano, was a clue that Alex had yet to link up to any motive. Remo being the co-owner of the law firm of Weitz & Romano based in New York, where Alex had enjoyed a decade-long stellar if not dubious career as a defense attorney.

After feeding Kibbles, Alex brought the dog with her to the sitting room and found a comfortable seat. Drinks had been set out—waters, sodas and a pot of tea with three porcelain tea cups and saucers.

Liam has thought of everything.

Alex skipped the drink and picked the most comfortable looking seat in the room—one she could curl up in.

"As I know the provenance of the American segment of the society, I can confirm neither Remo nor his sister Eleanor were ever members. There are a few logbooks and meeting notes, and those names weren't amongst the ones mentioned in the later years."

Reaching for the quilt on the back of her chair—a throw-sized grid of Greek Key blocks in scrappy blue and gray fabrics—Alex pulled it over her lap. Mulling over the conversation they'd been having she traced the pattern around and around to the dark center of the quilt block. Then she looked up. "Do you have any evidence that the firm in New York is connected?" Alex asked Liam, then covered her legs with the quilt and pulled it up under her chin.

"There's no proof, of course, or you would have uncovered it by now."

An ache in her heart caused her eyes to glaze as memories flooded her system—memories of the endless hours she and Hawk had spent trying to uncover clues or connections to Remo to explain Nona's murder.

"When we left Salem, the case of Eleanor Romano's demise was still open. And although Nona wasn't directly accused, mainly because she's deceased, I know she's the prime—well, only—suspect."

"That is a quandary indeed," Liam replied, sitting forward on the sofa.

"Was it Nona? Or my parents? Could they really be responsible for the woman's death?"

Unusually quiet, Charlotte sipped soda from a vintage cola bottle.

Liam clasped his hands. "I can't say for sure, but I believe it may have been a case of kill or be killed. It's possible all three of them were involved. Or none of them."

"But there were four unique fingerprints on the knife that killed Eleanor. Assuming my mom, dad and Nona, but who would the fourth person be?"

Charlotte jumped to her feet, the straw fell out of her soda bottle and Kibbles whined. "This is nuts. There's no way my grandmother . . . or your parents, were involved with murder." Charlotte bent and picked up the straw, then tossed it onto the coffee table.

Liam placed a napkin under the straw and gave Charlotte an apologetic frown.

Alex sighed. "I don't want to think about things like this either, but less than a year ago my old law firm's connection to the Mafia was just a suspicion. Then Nona was killed. Followed by the calamity on the cruise, leading to the second attempt on *my* life." Alex winced. "I thought I was leaving a high-profile life to return home to the peace and tranquility of my hometown, family, and quilting."

"Yeah, well, none of *that* happened," Charlotte muttered. "Speaking of quilting, you never showed us the quilting studio, Liam."

"Oh, yes, in the theater. I'll take you there first thing, when we head back over," Liam replied.

"The overarching pressing matter is clearing our family members' good names before anything else happens," Alex added, too exhausted to even think about quilting at this point.

"I quite agree." Liam stood and walked to the roll-top desk in the corner. He pulled out a file as Charlotte continued her speculation.

"Could this just be a cover-up? I hate these conspiracies, but I don't buy it. *Even if* Nona was doing all kinds of crazy things before her death. *Even if* she was leading an alternate life behind all our backs as a member of this secret society—which I'm still not a hundred percent sure of either."

"Not a member," Liam interrupted. "At the time of her passing, she was the head of the SOS."

"O-kay, the *leader*," Charlotte mocked.

"The term is actually Grand Quibah."

Alex eyed Liam as he stifled a grin, and she burst out laughing.

Kibbles stirred, from the comfortable spot she had chosen next to Charlotte on the sofa, both ears erect, the dog momentarily on guard.

"I know none of this is funny, but come on. Are you serious?" Alex asked, and grabbed for a tissue. She laughed so hard she needed to wipe her eyes and then blow her nose.

When Alex had regained her composure, Kibbles plonked her head back down and fell back asleep, snoring quietly.

"I admit, it was somewhat of a joke as to who came up with the name Quibah. An obvious play on words for a female quilter who becomes the Grand Poobah of a secret society."

"Nona came up with that, I'm sure." Charlotte shook her head.

"Yes, I'm sure she did," Liam replied, and adjusted his bow tie, his demeanor becoming somber momentarily.

"Okay, if we think Remo was responsible for taking out Nona and trying to—" Charlotte made an axing gesture across her neck, "—take out Alex."

Alex tucked the quilt tightly around her body and snuggled deeper into the enormous, cushy chair. "Yes, that was always our theory, but it just made little sense that after all this time, I, an accomplished lawyer, and my—well, Hawk, a skilled private investigator, couldn't find evidence to that fact."

Charlotte jammed the straw back into her bottle and slurped the last of her soda.

Gross. Doesn't she know there is no five-second, especially no five-minute, rule at someone else's house?

Charlotte set the bottle down a little too hard and asked, "What if it was a conspiracy?"

"Well, yes, that's obvious," Alex replied. She propped a throw pillow against the armrest and laid her head and arm over it.

"What if Remo took out his sister to gain the seat in the Society for himself by setting up Nona for the murder?" Charlotte asked.

Liam relaxed, crossing his legs. "No, that wouldn't work. Because the Society is just women. He wouldn't get in even if they let Eleanor in. It's more likely that it's not Remo you should be looking at."

"I can understand Remo not being allowed because he's a man, but why would his sister be precluded?" Alex asked.

"That, I believe, was a matter of preference, or preservation, on the part of the Society. The sitting members would've had to vote Eleanor in, and I suspect they were aware of her family's connection to the Mafia."

"But there's no proven connection, it's still all just speculation," Alex pointed out.

"Once you focus your attention in the right direction, I think you will see the web unravel."

"If you say so." Charlotte scoffed.

"But you said Alex's father was involved, and now you are. You are both men," Charlotte argued.

"Mere stewards of the wellspring," Liam replied with a serious face. "Not actual members. There's no way he, Remo, would think they'd give him the 'keeper of the secrets' job."

"Yeah, I guess that wouldn't make sense," Charlotte agreed.

"But if he wanted to *take over* the Society for himself, that could explain why he took out the Grand Quibah." Alex suppressed her feelings as the hilarity of Nona's behavior warred with the sadness of her passing.

A bell rang in the hallway, and Liam stood.

"Saved by the butler's bell," Charlotte cooed half-jokingly to Kibbles who was resting by her feet.

4

KIBBLES AND CHIRP FIND ROY

"That'll be the theater ringing." Liam checked his watch. "There's still a few hours before these night owls shut down for the evening. Shall we head back over and see their progress?"

"See the quilting studio?" Charlotte asked.

"Yes, of course."

"Let's go, snuggle bug," Charlotte teased Alex, who stood and folded the quilt, then draped it over the back of the chair where she'd found it.

The three left the main house with Kibbles cuddled in Charlotte's arms, and entered the theater through the rear exit. Chirp slinked in, weaving around Alex's feet. Kibbles jumped down. "Careful, that's a long drop, baby!" Alex called out.

Chirp waved his tail in Kibbles's face, taunting her. Then, Kibbles took the bait and gave chase. Chirp raced down the corridor, Kibbles skittering and bouncing off the wall as her feet failed to find purchase on the polished wooden floor. Chirp leapt onto a costume rack on wheels, sending it and the cat sliding down the hall, the dog and Liam in hot pursuit, until the rack crashed into a door at the end. The rack also slammed into the wall, bounced back, and toppled to the floor, burying both cat and dog in costumes. Alex and Charlotte stood gaping at the scene as Kibbles backed up, flinging off a red boa. The small dog bumped the ajar door with her rear end and it popped open.

Inside the now-open closet, a silhouette of a seated man slouched forward, landing face-first on the floor with a thud.

Alex bristled at the sight of the body splayed out on the floor in front of them. Though, she was no stranger to the sight of death—it was the déjà vu that upset her. A flashback hit her, of finding Nona in a nearly identical position when she'd been murdered just last spring.

As the group neared the body, Alex glanced around to determine what had happened. The deceased man clenched a pair of jeans in one hand, and a spool of thread rolled out of the other hand.

"Oh no," Liam cried out.

A slew of actors rushed to the hallway.

Charlotte, in her usual Captain Obvious style, said, "I bet we finally found Roy!"

"Well, actually, *Chirp and Kibbles* found Roy," Alex muttered.

Charlotte slouched, "The quilt studio will have to wait. Again."

Alex glared at her. *Priorities! Quilting isn't as important as a murder—though it's a close second.*

A woman nearly a foot taller than Alex, wearing a blonde wig, lurked over her shoulder and asked, "Who's going to sew our costumes now?"

All eyes focused on Alex and Charlotte, except for Emmie, who stood off to the side, glaring at the actress dressed as Marilyn Monroe.

"*We've* already told you. We're *quilters*," Charlotte snapped.

"I can do grommets," a man carrying a dog's head mask chimed in.

"That's not helpful, Wallace," Emmie snapped back. "Someone's murdered Roy."

The group let out a collective gasp.

An actor in an over-the-top Uncle Sam outfit, standing beside Alex said, "Look at all that blood."

"Was he shot?" Charlotte asked, standing on her tiptoes.

"Wouldn't someone have heard that?" one of the actors responded.

"Stabbed, I believe," Alex replied, while pulling her cell phone from her back pocket.

"By what?" the actor dressed as Uncle Sam asked.

"It's too dark. Can we get more light?" Alex pressed the home button, and the screen on her phone lit up just as the overhead lights brightened. She tapped 9.

"What are you doing?" Uncle Sam asked, standing a little too close for her comfort. He took off his hat and let out a deep breath.

"I'm calling this in. Someone needs to come and investigate his death, or murder, secure the crime scene and remove the body."

Emmie shrieked, "This is going to ruin our play!"

Charlotte rolled her eyes at the maligned assistant and scooped up Kibbles as she skidded by on some slick fabric.

Liam ushered the gaggle of actors to the other end of the hall and returned to Alex, putting his hand over her arm and asked, "Why don't we take this one? An investigation would, in fact, ruin the dedication events and play."

Charlotte shot Alex a look and whispered, "You know we really have to call the cops, right?"

Alex nodded.

Suzie, who hadn't gone with the other actors, cleared her

throat, and her gaze dropped to her shoes, which were covered in black fur. "We can call my uncle. He's a detective with the Mishap Police Department. I'm sure he'll be discreet."

Charlotte gave Alex a questioning glance.

"We have Alex and Charlotte here. They're detectives," Liam replied.

"Wait, what?" Charlotte balked. "We're *not* detectives."

Alex shuffled uncomfortably. "She's right."

"I'm sure my uncle would appreciate your help."

Charlotte laughed. "I doubt that."

Alex put out her hand to settle her friend. "Okay, fine. Call your uncle, and we'll *help* him."

The lights flickered, and the dimly lit hallway brightened as the overhead fluorescents turned up. Suzie made the phone call to her uncle, whispering with her hand covering her mouth. Her eyes darted to Alex, and she nodded.

What is she up to?

Liam walked back toward the cast members. "We called for a detective to help us handle this in a discreet manner."

"But if there's a murderer on the loose, aren't *we* in danger?" the actress dressed as Marilyn Monroe asked.

"No. No. Please, just relax, the investigator will arrive soon. We'll all stay together here with each other until he does. We'll be just fine."

"But what if it's one of us?" Suzie asked.

Charlotte turned back, headed toward their original destination. "We might as well go visit the quilt studio while we wait."

"Charlotte!" Alex hooked her at the elbow, holding her back. "You certainly are Nona's granddaughter."

With a pleading expression, Liam said, "Please, Charlotte, let's stick together for now. There will be plenty of time for that later."

Not even ten minutes later, a man dressed in a shabby

suit, wearing a distressed fedora entered the theater from an ominous passageway opposite the stage that Alex hadn't even realized was there. *The detective we're supposed to be 'helping'?*

"Look, it's a vomitory, Alex! We'll have to scope that out later." Charlotte grinned.

A what?

As if she read her mind, or maybe Alex's face just gave away her confusion, Charlotte replied, "Just a fancy word for an entrance piercing the banks of seats of a theater, amphitheater, or stadium."

"You have the definition memorized?"

"No, I just looked it up on the internet!" Charlotte replied, shaking her head at Alex.

The detective approached the group. "My name's Little, Detective Seymour Little." He tipped his finger-stained fedora.

"You must be Alex?" he asked, and extended his hand.

Alex shook his hand and answered, "Yes. And this is Charlotte, we—"

Turning to Charlotte, he said, "The sleuths my niece mentioned on the phone." He turned back and handed Alex his business card.

Alex glanced at the card, put it in her pants pocket and eyed him with a puzzled expression. *What is this guy's shtick?*

"Suzie has explained Roy was discovered in the costume closet, is that correct?" The detective spoke to the group huddled by the stage.

"No, the janitor's closet," Emmie corrected, her eyes darting toward the hallway.

"Well, then I guess we should start with the janitor."

"We don't have a janitor, sir," Liam replied, but his tone was casual.

Do they know each other?

"Well, let's start with a coffee, Mr.—" The detective held out his hand again.

"Liam Arnold. You can call me Liam."

I guess they don't know each other?

"Oh, yes, Suzie has told me so much about your work here with the students and the theater. The renovations are spot on."

The detective peered around, rubbing his hands together. "Let's have a look at the poor fellow who met his untimely demise, shall we? And that coffee?"

"Yes, Emmie will happily fetch you a cup. Right this way."

Emmie grimaced as the detective and Liam walked away. Liam guided the detective down the hall to where they'd found Roy.

Emmie scurried off in the opposite direction. She paused and looked back just before stepping out of sight.

"I don't like her," Charlotte murmured, surveying Emmie's every move.

"I'm sure she's just flustered having to get coffee while one of her fellow actors lies dead in the closet," Alex replied, and the two women followed the detective and Liam. The remaining actors traipsed along behind them like an entourage.

Charlotte still carried Kibbles. "I'm not sure what Seymour Little's angle is here. But I'm not sure I'll be much help in the amateur sleuth department. I can barely manage my own life."

"Just keep your eyes open and look for any loose threads." Alex chuckled nervously.

"There *seam* to be a lot of loose threads here already," Charlotte replied with a wicked grin.

Alex reached for Kibbles. "Let me take her, I don't want her getting down and running around the crime scene." She relieved Charlotte of the dog.

Kibbles thanked Alex by licking her in the ear, her tail wagging rapidly.

"Yuck."

The detective yelled, "Someone catch that cat!"

A flash of orange blurred by, as Chirp scooted by Liam who caught only a handful of fur from the exceptionally fast feline. The tomcat weaved around between everyone's feet, expertly avoiding capture before vanishing into the darkness.

"Good luck catching that tabby," Charlotte scoffed.

Emmie appeared with coffee.

"Ah, thank you." Liam reached out for the coffee and handed it off to the detective. Standing just feet away from Roy's slumped figure, the detective pulled off the cover of the cup. A hint of Colombian dark roast filled the air, and he sniffed appreciatively.

"Thank you, warms the bones." He sipped the coffee. "*My* bones, of course."

Charlotte leaned in to whisper to Alex. "Who is this guy?"

Alex shrugged. She wasn't entirely sure who this detective was, or what his peculiar unkempt style was all about: a brown stain on his tie; his shirt partially untucked; but his fedora, while broken in and well worn, was expensive and perfectly poised on his freshly cut salt-and-pepper hair. His mustache and beard were both combed and meticulously groomed.

Whatever this guy's contradictions are, I'll be watching him.

5

IT'S BEEN A LONG DAY!

DETECTIVE LITTLE SET HIS COFFEE DOWN ON THE SHELF inside the closet and then turned to the group. "Excuse me, ladies and gentlemen. I need to secure this area. Please, everyone, step back."

The actors huddled backward, grumbling under their breath.

"Did anyone find any evidence, or disturb the body?"

"Only you," Charlotte mumbled. "He just put his coffee in the closet, in the crime scene," she said in a low voice, with a horrified look on her face. "Even I know better than to do that."

There's nothing I can say. She's right.

Examining the area around the body, he stepped too close.

"What is he doing?" Charlotte asked in an exasperated tone. "He almost put his foot in the pool of blood."

Taking no notice of Charlotte and her outrage, the detective continued, "Was there a struggle? Does anyone know how the victim ended up in this closet?"

"Isn't he supposed to tell us the answers to those questions?" the Marilyn Monroe actress asked. *She* hadn't bothered to lower her voice, or whisper.

A shutter click pinged behind Alex, and she turned to catch the Uncle Sam actor sneaking a picture of the body. "What are you doing? Don't—"

"Excuse me, ah, sir," Detective Little stuttered. "If we are to keep this discreet, no pictures please. I'm going to have to ask you to delete that."

Uncle Sam stepped back, looking embarrassed, tapped the screen several times and hid his cell phone behind his back.

The detective continued his examination of the scene. He scribbled notes onto a small leatherbound pad. "Alex, why don't *we* snap a couple images of the body and crime scene."

"Doesn't he have a phone he can take his own pictures with?" Charlotte said, her voice low but rising.

Alex shot her a warning look and then walked around Roy's body, careful not to get too close, capturing pictures from all angles, when she finally saw the murder weapon—scissors, dressmaker's *shears* to be exact.

Alex snapped several more photos of the scissors protruding from Roy's jugular—as well as photos of the closet interior—before tucking her phone into her back pocket.

She spied the Uncle Sam actor backing away suspiciously as if no one would notice.

Wiping sweat from his brow, Seymour cleared his throat. He faced the group of actors. "You must all stay here."

Uncle Sam paused his retreat just as the actor dressed as a bloodhound turned pale and passed out. If not for Harrison stepping forward and catching him, the costumed guy would have landed hard on the floor.

"Should we call an ambulance for Wallace?" Emmie asked, sidling up between Alex and Charlotte.

Suzie rushed to Wallace's side just as Harrison set the bloodhound actor down carefully. "No, no. He has vasovagal syncope, he just needs to put his legs up for a few minutes.

Someone get him a pillow that he can prop his legs up with. Oh, and one for his head too."

Wallace mumbled, "I'm fine. I'll just lie down for a little while."

"Okay, folks. Nothing to see there. I'll need your attention, please. I'm going to need to ask you all a few questions," the detective said. He asked Liam, "Is there somewhere private we can go for interviews?"

"Yes. There's some empty space in the dressing room area. Right this way," Liam said, and ushered him through a set of burgundy velvet curtains.

"Who is this guy?" Charlotte questioned again.

"Let's just go with it until we have a chance to break out on our own," Alex replied.

Charlotte's eyes bugged. "Like right now?"

"I'm not sure that would be appropriate. I don't want him to start sniffing around us." Alex raised her eyebrows, teasing.

Liam passed back through the curtains and called for the Marilyn Monroe actress, whose name, Alex learned, was Jojo, and sent her into the makeshift interrogation area.

Liam approached Charlotte, Alex, and Kibbles, who was now squirming frantically to get out of Alex's arms.

"Liam, I need to take her out, now, sorry."

"Sure, sure, let's the three of us step outside for a moment with Kibbles."

Alex led the way. Behind her, Charlotte asked Liam, "He knows *we're* not detectives, right?"

A gust of cold air hit them as they opened the backstage door. Kibbles whined, Alex set her down, and Kibbles ran to the nearest 'tree,' which was a dog-sized ornamental bush.

"Yes, I explained that you are only *amateur sleuths*."

Kibbles shot past them, doing zoomies around the courtyard, circling two pots of pink and purple hellebores.

Charlotte walked toward the house. "No, we really aren't. At least I'm not. I'm just a cashier at my local Pop and Shop."

After a brief intermission, allowing for Kibbles to do her business, they all returned to the theater. She eyed Emmie leading one of the actors through the curtains. Gold tassels hung off to the side to tie the curtains back.

"What are you doing?" Alex asked her.

"We're going to question Harrison now," Emmie replied.

Charlotte walked up carrying the cat, Chirp, after sweet-talking him off the front porch of the house. "We?" She questioned.

"Yes, we," Emmie replied. "I'm his representative."

Alex took a step toward Emmie. "Are you a lawyer in the real world?"

Emmie blinked repeatedly. "Well, no. But I've played one on stage–I'm an actress!" Emmie huffed. Her overalls made a scratching noise as she stormed off and went to sit beside Suzie on the deck of the stage. A rack of unusual costumes hung behind them, and she swatted at a dress that's tassels kept hanging in her face.

"Have you been wondering what kind of play this is?" Charlotte asked Alex.

"Yes. It's pretty strange for Uncle Sam, Marilyn Monroe, and who's that?" Alex pointed to a balding man.

"I think that's supposed to be Alfred Hitchcock." Charlotte

cackled. "No seriously, it's *Detective Seymour Little*," Charlotte said mockingly.

"I didn't recognize him from behind, and without the fedora. He's balding on the back of his head."

"Maybe you should get your eyes checked when we get home?" Charlotte teased.

Alex ignored her. "Do we know what part Roy was to play?"

"No, I don't think anyone has mentioned it. Maybe James Dean?" Charlotte chortled.

Alex laughed. "You're full of it today, aren't you."

"I'm anxious to get into that quilting studio."

"Soon enough. Be patient." Alex replied, as Charlotte bounced on the balls of her feet.

"I'm surprised you know who Alfred Hitchcock is. I didn't think you watched old movies."

Charlotte winked. "Might help us with the investigation."

Alex groaned in reply. "I'd rather *not* be investigating, especially when we have a *detective* here to do that." Alex leaned toward Charlotte and lowered her voice. "I'd much rather dig into this secret society business."

"Or get into the quilt studio!"

Alex laughed. "You're hopeless."

"Woof!" Kibbles wrapped her head and paws around Alex's neck.

"Kibbles agrees!"

"Do you really believe in this 'detective'?" Charlotte peered through the curtains.

A commotion caught their attention.

Someone yelled, "He's choking."

Alex jumped up and, right behind Charlotte, rushed through the velvet curtain separating them from the dressing rooms. "It's the detective, he's choking!" Charlotte yelled.

Harrison, the guy in charge of lighting and sound, jumped

behind Detective Little and into a position to do the Heimlich maneuver.

"I can't breathe, I'm choking," Seymour Little yelled, holding his throat with one hand and his coffee cup in the other.

"But you're talking," Harrison responded, and stopped his life-saving acting. "I guess that means I've saved you!"

"But you didn't do anything," Emmie argued, standing beside them with her hands tucked into the top of her overalls.

The detective recovered instantaneously and miraculously. "I think it's time to call the coroner to pick up the body."

"Well, that was a fast recovery," Charlotte said, scowling.

Detective Little pulled his cell phone from his pocket, dialed and turned his back on the group. After a hushed conversation he snapped his ancient flip phone shut.

"Now that's taken care of, what's next?" he asked, looking pointedly at Alex and then glancing at Charlotte.

"Sleep!" Charlotte replied.

Liam approached. "Ladies, you're right. It's terribly late, and there isn't much else we can do here. Detective, we have a rooms prepared in the main house. Join us. And Suzie is welcome also."

"Yes, of course. Hopefully it won't take long for the coroner to pick up the body. Plus, it will give me a chance to investigate further."

The detective scribbled in his notepad and guzzled his coffee. "What exactly is the difference between scissors and shears? Aren't they the same thing?" he asked.

Charlotte gaped. "Seriously, that's like calling a quilt a blanket!"

"No it's not. Stop it, Charlotte. Technically shears *are* scissors, but they have differences, like shears have two different-sized handles, whereas regular scissors have both handles the same size."

"Fascinating!" the detective replied, and tucked his notepad into his ratty dress shirt pocket. "Do we know where the pets were at the time of death?"

Charlotte scoffed. "Does it matter? They don't have fingers to use shears or scissors, unless they teamed up. Maybe Chirp held them while Kibbles jabbed Roy." Charlotte rolled her eyes.

Alex pinched her, whispering, "Seriously, Charlotte?"

"What? It's as good a theory as the last one, or the next."

Alex shook her head at the ridiculousness.

6

THE SHOW MUST GO ON

The next morning, Alex and Charlotte enjoyed a lavish breakfast with Liam. "This is too much. You shouldn't have," Alex said, piling a heaping scoop of peach cobbler onto her plate from the chafing dish.

"I don't mind at all," Charlotte said, crunching on a piece of bacon.

Alex and Charlotte sat at the twelve-person dining room table lined with elegant Parsons chairs. "I'm not waiting for the detective," Charlotte said, before stuffing a mini blueberry muffin into her mouth.

"No need," Alex replied, and flashed her eyes toward the door as Liam stood in greeting as the detective entered the dining room and wandered to the window, oblivious to the breakfast spread. Liam sat back down.

"Have some breakfast," Alex said getting the detective's attention and then gesturing to the buffet.

"Well, don't mind if I do." He rubbed his stomach, and walked over to the coffee bar. Seymour poured himself a cup and clinked a spoon in the coffee mug, stirring in creamer and then a heaping spoonful of sugar.

"Did the coroner pick up the deceased last night?" Alex asked.

"They're coming his morning." Little replied

Alex shot Charlotte a sidelong glance. "The body was left in the theater overnight?"

"I secured the scene before I retired to bed."

"Is that how long it usually takes?" Charlotte scoffed with a look of disdain.

"It's a small town, and everyone was out of town for a wedding." The detective shrugged, "but most everyone's returning today, just in time for the play."

Charlotte glared at him, her eyebrows scrunched in disapproval.

"The show must go on!" Liam spoke to no one in particular. "Many influential people will indeed be arriving in Mishap for the show."

"Liam? You're going to go on with the play?" Alex questioned before drinking her juice.

"Ladies, ladies, *the show must go on*," Liam repeated, pouring himself a tall glass of milk from a carafe. "If for no other reason than because we need the publicity."

"And the money, I suspect," the detective added, and sat next to Charlotte.

Alex mouthed, 'I think he likes you.'

Liam cleared his throat. "Yes, certainly. The money will be a significant benefit to the theater and the artists. They have put a lot of hard work into preparing for the show."

Suzie entered the room. "What about the bad publicity of a dead person, the scandal of murder, or the danger of a murderer on the loose?" Suzie asked. "Uncle." She bent to give the detective a peck on his left cheek.

"Niece. Good morning. I hope you slept well, dear."

"I did. The rooms here are grand, aren't they?" Suzie said, looking to Alex for an affirmative agreement.

"Yes, quite comfortable. I fell right to sleep. Though, I would have liked a few more hours," she replied.

"I don't think there is any worry of the news of the victim's untimely death getting out. I know the coroner. He's very professional," the detective replied to Suzie's earlier question. "Though, for everyone's safety we do need to go back over to the theater and catch this culprit quickly."

After breakfast, Alex dressed Kibbles in a fresh sweater and took her for their morning walk through the courtyard. The powerful scent and purple coloring of the hyacinths reminded Alex of the lilac bushes flanking number 1 Spruce Street.

Chirp lurked under the bench and swatted at Kibbles as she trotted by, causing her to jump and skitter off.

"Woof, woof, woof." Her little pink tongue hung out of her mouth as she panted.

"Kibbles, come!" Alex set down a small collapsible water dish and filled it from a water bottle in her bag.

Charlotte walked up, picked up the skittish pup and soothed her. "Now, now. Did that big cat scare you?"

"That cat is twice her size," Alex said through a laugh.

"Alex, this is a dumpster fire. Worse than the way things are handled back home?" Charlotte asked. She set Kibbles on the bench and sat.

Alex sat beside them. "I don't know."

Charlotte pulled her winter hat down over her ears. "I searched for the detective on the internet last night. He's not on the police website. No social media presence either. He acts no more like a detective than we do."

Alex stroked Kibbles and watched Chirp chase a little field mouse through the square. "There's not much we can do. This is their business."

"Well—" Charlotte began.

"Don't say it, I know. The quilt studio."

"Ha, ha. I'm so curious. Aren't you?"

"I guess." Alex tucked one hand into her coat pocket for warmth, and brushed against something metal—the three keys. "But you know what puzzles me? Who are the six people in the Society of Six? It doesn't add up."

"Does anything about Nona add up?"

"Not lately," Alex replied.

Charlotte stood and flipped the hood of her sweatshirt over her hat. "Let's head over to the theater. And see what Captain Obvious, I mean Detective *See-less*, is up to this morning." Charlotte erupted in uncontrollable laughter.

"What are you, twelve?"

Charlotte carried Kibbles, and Chirp followed them in, racing between their feet as the humans hopped around trying to avoid stepping on the plump cat.

The detective was on a phone call, pacing around, nodding. "Well, as I suspected, the dead body is dead, and he was still warm when we arrived. The most likely suspect is yet to show him or herself." He looked up at Alex, Kibbles and Charlotte and then slapped his flip phone shut. "Good morning, ladies," the detective greeted.

Charlotte exclaimed, "Again!"

"That was the coroner. Letting me know EMTs from nearby Misfortune will be picking up the body."

Mishap, Misfortune? I'm guessing this area has a rich history! Alex chuckled to herself.

"I'm just going to call him CO, you know, for Captain Obvious, from now on," Charlotte said. This time her 'whisper' was a little less conspicuous.

Ignoring Charlotte's rude comment, the detective continued, "The man, Roy, was most certainly killed with the dressmaking shears. We have no viable suspects so far, so I will continue to investigate, and you two can just go about your business here."

"Finally, the quilt studio!" Charlotte bounced, and a smile lit up her face. Charlotte's excitement was quickly overshadowed by the EMT's arrival and departure. Within minutes they were wheeling Roy out on a gurney. Charlotte pointed and asked the detective, "Shouldn't we go with them?"

"Nah, you little ladies stay here. Show me those crime scene photos, won't ya," he said.

Alex fished her phone out of her back pocket and pulled up the images. She handed the phone to the detective. "Just swipe left."

He reviewed the pictures. "Yes, as I suspected, scissors to the jugular."

"Okay, Captain Obvious," Charlotte mumbled, still holding Kibbles.

The detective returned Alex's phone and proclaimed, "I've determined no one here had access to those scissors."

"Actually, didn't *everyone* have access to those *shears*?" Alex rebutted.

"Well, everyone except you and me, because conceivably we weren't here at the time of the murder," Charlotte interjected.

Seymour flipped through his notepad. "According to Emmie's account, the three of you *were* here prior to leaving and then coming back."

"I guess, depending on the timeline. But why do you say no one here had access to the dressmaker's shears?" Alex asked.

"Precisely!" he replied.

"Precisely what?" Charlotte questioned.

He pursed his lips, "No one here was a sewer, and the only tailor is now dead."

Charlotte shook her head. "I think you're taking the *cardinal rule—Thou shalt not use fabric scissors for anything other than cutting fabric*—to the ultimate extreme."

Alex laughed, and Kibbles barked in agreement. "It makes more sense that a troupe full of non-sewers *would* use the scissors as a murder weapon. And the only person or persons who *wouldn't* would be the sewers," she argued.

"And the quilters," Charlotte added, pointing between herself and Alex.

"You can rule Charlotte and Alex out, they don't have motive." Suzie said, sidling up alongside her uncle.

"Well, the only person we can truly rule out is the owner of the scissors, Roy, as he's deceased," Detective Little replied.

"How does he even know those are Roy's scissors?" Charlotte asked and wrinkled her brows. "Surely *we* can do better than *this guy*," she continued whispering.

"I think we might have to step in after all." Alex reached for her phone. "Maybe I should call Hawk to come down and help us investigate?"

Charlotte stopped her by grabbing her arm. "Let's you and I see this one through. We can always consult with him later if we need to. Come on, Alex, it'll be fun to team up on this."

"I don't think fun is the right word, Charlotte."

"Wait, Uncle, I think there's a clue you may be overlooking." Suzie interjected.

"Eureka?" Charlotte exclaimed sarcastically.

"The killer must either be right-handed or ambidextrous."

The detective tapped his lips with his index finger. "And you think this why?"

"The scissors were jammed into Roy's neck on the right," Suzie offered.

"Right-handed scissors," Charlotte mumbled.

"Well, let's start with you two, shall we? Are either of you right-handed?"

"Well, I am," Alex replied, waving her right hand. "But so is at least eighty percent of the population."

"Including the dog!" Charlotte added, holding up one of Kibbles's paws.

Alex stifled a laugh and asked her, "What makes you say that?"

Charlotte shrugged and put the dog down. "She always lifts her right leg."

"I don't think that's even a thing."

"Okay, well . . . as we said previously, we're quilters. We know better than to use *fabric scissors* for anything other than *cutting fabric*. Never mind using them as a murder weapon," Charlotte added. "Would never happen." She then waved her left hand. "Left-handed, by the way."

Emmie floated by with a tray full of coffees. The detective reached out, but she didn't stop to offer him one.

"Well, I'll take that under careful consideration," the detective replied, and scribbled in his notepad, then walked away.

"Where are you going?" Charlotte asked.

"To test this right-handed theory of yours, Suzie. Of course," he called back over his shoulder before disappearing behind the velvet curtains.

"Should we follow him?" Charlotte asked.

Kibbles barked her signature no, "Woof, woof."

"Well, I think I'm going to have to disagree with you on this one, Kibbles. Let's see how he *tests* her theory," Alex replied to both Kibbles and Charlotte.

Alex ducked through the curtains to the dressing area. The

space was nothing more than a storage warehouse, cordoned off by tall metal racks and more velvet curtains.

"Everyone, please let me have your attention. Stop talking. I need you to step up to this line here." The detective swept his foot along an imaginary line drawn in the dust on the concrete floor.

"One at a time. Please, you first. What is your name, ma'am?"

Emmie, at the front of the pack, said, "Emmie, I'm the one who *fetches* your coffee."

"Nice. And thank you. Please write your name here in this notepad and then wink at me."

"Say what? I just told you my name. And what kind of ridiculous request is that—wink at you?"

"Just do as you're asked, Emmie. Please," Liam said from behind Alex. Alex turned and let Liam through between her and Charlotte as Detective Little bumbled through his test.

Emmie used her left hand to write her name and winked at him with her left eye.

One by one, each member of the cast stepped up to the line and signed their name and winked at the detective.

"Fine, you may all go about your business now."

The actors dispersed, and the detective asked Liam to perform his test.

Liam signed with his left hand and winked with his right eye.

"Is this everyone who was here yesterday?" Detective Little asked Liam, and displayed the notepad.

"Well, yes, this's everyone, but that"—Liam pointed to the notepad—"is illegible."

"Inconclusive. The results of the test are inconclusive." Seymour paced in a wide arc around Alex, Charlotte, and Liam.

"Why inconclusive?" Charlotte asked.

"Everyone here is left-handed. Except Alex, and Liam, who appears to be ambidextrous." He stopped pacing and stared at Alex, wide eyed.

"How is that even possible? Isn't being left-handed rare?" Charlotte asked.

"Yes, it's more likely that everyone except my niece and Liam would be right-handed," he replied to Charlotte.

"And the dog." Charlotte barked.

She's certainly giving this guy a hard time.

Kibbles batted a small pompom past them and Alex cringed, momentarily distracted from the conversation. *I hope she didn't chew that off a costume.*

Another thought occurred to her. "If the person stabbed Roy from behind, wouldn't that make them left-handed?" Alex suggested. She tugged out her cell phone and pulled up the picture of Roy. "Suzie was mistaken. We were looking at Roy, and the scissors *were* sticking out on the right side, but that is actually *his* left side."

Charlotte peered at the photo. "How about the two handles, would that help us make the determination?"

"I don't think so. If you held the shears in either hand, the small handle would be up," Alex replied to Charlotte.

"Or down." Charlotte pretended to have shears in her hand and made striking motions. "You would cut with the small handle up, but if you were going to jab with them, the small handle would be down." She jabbed her imaginary shears a couple more times. "Or sideways, actually."

The detective watched Charlotte's act with a curious look on his face, "As I said, inconclusive."

"Oh, I can't take any more of this guy," Charlotte complained, and stormed out. Kibbles tried to follow Charlotte as she bailed, but Alex scooped her up and tucked the pup under her arm.

"What's your plan now, Detective?" Alex asked. She was a thread's width away from walking out just like Charlotte had.

He threw his finger up in the air. "We must take a serious look at these pets."

Alex shot him a grumpy expression, but set Kibbles down to walk on her own. Kibbles stood still, staring up at Alex like putting her down was a sin. "Come on Kibbs, let's go baby."

Now, I've *had enough of this guy.* "It seems like Charlotte and I are needed back at the main house. If you'll excuse us." She shot Liam an apologetic look before walking out.

7

SOS

ALEX AND CHARLOTTE STOOD WARMING THEIR HANDS OVER the fireplace in the sitting room, the mantel exquisitely carved. The glow of the afternoon sun was replaced by evening firelight and flickering candles around the room.

"I can't believe he wants to investigate the pets. That guy's a crackpot, Alex."

Liam entered silently and sat in the wingback chair. Kibbles was snoring quietly on the opposite sofa.

"Liam, who are the six members of the Society of Six?" Alex asked, still chewing on the information Liam revealed the day before. "The math doesn't add up. Nona, my mom and dad, you . . . ? Who else?"

Liam chortled. "As I said, we—the men—weren't really considered part of the six. But honestly, as far as I can discern there never were six at any one given time, here in the US. Maybe they had six originally, or maybe the name really was supposed to be SOS?" He grinned. It was obvious to Alex he was pleased with himself.

Alex sat on the oversized chaise, these chairs were quickly

becoming her favorite spots—each large enough to curl up on with a comfy quilt.

I should order one of these for number 1.

Liam continued, "The men were never members, though we had our jobs. I was the Society's lawyer, while your dad was the keeper."

I hadn't realized he was a lawyer also.

She practiced the avoidance technique when it came to dealing with losing her parents. She didn't speak of them often —they'd been taken from her too soon, when she was just fifteen.

"The founding member of the Society, as far as I know it—was Winnefred Winters."

"Oh yes, I know that name. I have a quilt with her name on it. Actually, it says Rebecca Briggs, but they're the same person. It's the last one I need to deliver from the pile Nona left. My friend, well, he's a private investigator, Hawk, did some research on the name. Winnefred emigrated from London at a young age, around 1960, and lived in New York for five years before she changed her name to Rebecca Briggs and dropped off the grid."

"Yes, that information aligns with what I know," Liam replied. "She's as far as we go back. We have no records of who the other original members of the six were. Although there is a document that references a duchess, Duchess of Snodsbury."

"That's a funny title," Charlotte commented. She stroked Kibbles as Chirp sat by the fire chirping out a conversation the humans couldn't understand.

"Do you know Rebecca Briggs, Liam? She must be your age? Or older."

"No. I have no more information than your PI friend gave you. Winnefred, or Rebecca if you prefer, would be slightly younger than Nona and me, by about five or so years."

Alex was envisioning a timeline in her head, which froze when Charlotte changed topics.

"Why did Henrietta think you were Nona's second love, Liam?"

"Besides your grandfather, Nona's only other love was for sleuthing. I was just the cover—she used my name to explain away her secrets to Henrietta."

"What do you mean, sleuthing? I know she was a bit of a busybody, thinking she was the matriarch of the neighborhood, but—" Alex questioned.

"Nona was quite the traveler. She and her friend Pauline found themselves, or probably more accurately *inserted* themselves amidst a murder case or mystery every time they vacationed. I think she was intending on writing a book about her adventures. You should check her journals."

"They're coded. Do you know how to decode them?" Alex asked.

"Of course, I am the key." Liam flashed a dimpled grin at Alex.

He's not really butler-like. I can't put my finger on who he reminds me of.

"But how? What exactly does that mean?" Charlotte asked.

Liam leaned forward, beckoning Alex and Charlotte to do the same. "Metaphorically, I am the key because I am the keeper of the secret society's information. Practically, I am the key to Nona's coded journals as well—LIAM. It's a substitution cipher. I'll give it to you before you leave, Alex."

"We totally should've figured that one out!" Charlotte laughed.

"This all seems like something out of the *National Treasure* or *Da Vinci Code* movies. I just don't understand how Nona lived such a full life, and we had no knowledge of any of it," Alex said, still regretful she hadn't been able to stop Nona's murder—and given the life-size statue now residing on Alex's lawn, she would be unlikely to let those feelings go anytime soon.

"Or anything about *her*," Charlotte added, her voice cold. She traced the hexagon quilt blocks made by Nona, on the table mat that was beside her.

Alex bristled at Charlotte's tone. The two had worked out their squabble during the charity quilting event, but Alex was wary of the wedge of jealousy driving them further apart. Nona was Charlotte's biological grandmother, but Alex had always been closer to Nona than Charlotte was.

"Are there any other properties Nona bought, that you know of, Liam?"

"No, I can't say that I am aware of any."

Alex snuggled back into the cushions of the chaise. "That's a relief."

Liam answered Alex's earlier question. "As to why you never knew Nona's activities, when you two were younger, you were both in school; you may have known and didn't realize at the time. Then you grew up with your own lives. Alex attended law school and moved to New York and . . ."

Alex frowned, her heart heavy. "But we're grown now. Why keep it from us still? Why hide her travels and her friends?"

"She was protecting you, Alex. Both of you, really. It's not called a secret society for nothing." Liam smiled, the smile Alex was sure melted many women's hearts in his day. His expression changed as though he was dwelling on a fond memory. "She was a very private person, you know."

Alex nodded. "It still feels like she was two different people, the no-nonsense Nona we knew and the flight-of-fancy woman embroidered in murder, mystery and intrigue."

"And danger!" Charlotte added.

"Okay, so, Nona and my mother were members. And my

father was a 'keeper'? What does that mean?" Alex kicked off her own shoes before putting her feet up. She wrapped her arms around her knees, pondering all the information.

"As the keeper, like I am now, your father did all the research. Nona had brought in your parents."

"But, how did Nona get involved?" Charlotte questioned.

Kibbles stirred and barked a low alarm call in her sleep, "Woof, woof, woof."

"Shh, baby, it's okay." Alex tilted her head and asked, "Wait, where did they used to keep all of this stuff that is now down stairs?" Alex asked.

Liam answered Charlotte first, "To the best of my knowledge she entered the Society through your grandmother, Alex. Your grandmother never wanted your mother, Fiona, to get involved, the same as how your families never wanted either of you to get involved. And as to where the memorabilia was kept —on Spruce Street of course." Liam shrugged and added, "there wasn't quite as much of it previously, of course. I'm a bit of a connoisseur."

"How? Where?" Alex asked.

"There's a room under number 1."

Charlotte blurted out, "Say what?"

Alex blew out a deep breath. "Is that what the keys go to?"

"No, I'm certain they don't." Liam replied and mumbled, "I wonder if they will open any physical object at all."

"I'm not sure which of those subjects to question first?" Alex replied. "How do we," Alex eyed Charlotte and pointed between the two of them, "not know about a secret room in my own house?"

As kids, she and Charlotte ran wild around the old Victorian, playing dress up, acting like princesses, and playing countless games of hide and seek.

Liam sat back and crossed his legs. "Same as we have here, wouldn't you think?" He flashed Alex a coy smile.

"You're not going to tell us?" Alex asked, and pulled another quilt off the back of the chair, wrapped it around her legs and waited for Liam's reply. She ran her fingers over the bold floral patterns on a classic Grandmother's Flower Garden quilt. An ache burned deep in her heart as she thought about Nona's quilting and her fabric stash.

"Well, with any secret society there is always a bit of intrigue, mystery..."

Great, where's the secret room?

Liam continued, still not answering her question. "...and of course danger. Otherwise what would be the point of the secret society?"

He winked. I saw it. Definitely not butler-like. What a devil, leaving me hanging like that.

Alex peered around the room, wondering where a secret wall, or hidden passage might be in her own house. Instead, she noticed the small touches of Nona everywhere her eyes landed: quilted table mats, a hand-embroidered pillow, and even a quilted pet bed for Chirp—which he'd clearly grown out of since it was created. "Do you think Roy's murder has anything to do with the secret society?"

Liam stiffened. "I should hope not. Though, I haven't ruled it out in my mind. I can protect you, I assure. I'm a skilled fighter. Don't let my age fool you."

Charlotte giggled, and Alex glared at her before responding to Liam. "I'm sure we won't need you to protect us, but we appreciate the sentiment."

Alex reached out to the small brass knob on the drawer of the side table. *I bet there's a sewing kit in there.* She looked to Charlotte, who was sending her a 'go for it' vibe. She quickly released her hand. *I better not, I don't want to be rude.*

The huge marmalade cat rubbed against Liam's leg, caterwauling his dismay. Liam casually wiped a few stray hairs off his pant leg.

"Meeeow! Chirp, chirp, chirp."

"Woof, woof, woof." Kibbles shot to her feet, firing off her warning alarm in response to Chirp's. Her ears flattened against her head.

"It seems my feline friend is unhappy," Liam said. He bent to run his thin hand down the length of the cat's back.

"And my canine companion senses danger," Alex added, and laughed as Kibbles trotted over to the cat and sniffed it. "Come, Kibbles." Alex leaned over and clapped for the dog.

A thick double paw swatted the air past where the dog's nose would've been, but Kibbles was quicker and she darted away just in time.

"Woof, woof."

The cat let out a soft "chirp."

Charlotte pursed her lips. "If I didn't know better, I'd say the pets are talking to each other."

"Oh yes, indeed they are. They speak the same language," Liam admitted. His face showed no insincerity.

Charlotte laughed. "How's that even possible?"

"They've both been trained the same."

"But how?" Alex questioned, eyeing the cat as it stretched out his claws on a small braided rug. "Was Kibbles's previous owner, Lilith, a member of the Society?"

"No, of course not. That madwoman *was* part of the Mafia. That I'm sure of."

"So Remo hired her," Alex mumbled.

"I'd say not. It's funny that people always think men run the Mafia." Liam shook his head and grinned. "In this case, I think you'll make more progress on your investigations if you start looking at the 'Comare.'"

"What does that word mean?" Charlotte asked, a confused look on her face. Kibbles stood on her hind legs, and Charlotte picked her up. The pooch made herself comfortable in Charlotte's lap and closed her eyes.

"The word means 'Godmother,'" Liam replied matter-of-factly.

"Oh, I get it, like Godfather." Charlotte stroked Kibbles's back, smiling. "And the pets?" Charlotte asked. Chirp, busy preening himself, paid no attention to the two-legged humans, and Kibbles's little legs were running in the air as she dreamed.

"The original pet sleuth was a royal corgi. Cousin to the queen's own. We found that even a stray mutt or chirping cat could be trained just the same. There's a training manual. I'll get it for you before you leave."

"So they are both trained to communicate and aid with solving crimes?" Charlotte asked.

Alex smiled. *Having learned exactly how Kibbles communicates does make things easier for me as a pet parent.* "But how was Kibbles trained, if her previous owner, Lilith, wasn't part of the Society of Six?"

"It's puzzling, isn't it? I suspect—"

Liam was cut off when a rush of wind, howling like a wolf, burst through the room. Seconds later the front door slammed, and Detective Little entered the sitting room, rubbing his hands together as he blew on them.

"It sure is chilly. Am I interrupting anything?"

Charlotte slid to the edge of the sofa, as if ready to bolt out of the room at the sight of the fumbling detective. To her credit, she didn't. Kibbles, however, jumped off Charlottes lap and was on all fours—bellowing her three-alarm call.

"Shh, stop, Kibbles, please. There's no danger, it's just the detective."

8

I'LL DO IT. NO, YOU DO IT

Charlotte cooed. Kibbles moved back to her side, and Charlotte stroked the dog until she was calm again.

"How are you coming along with the investigation, Detective? Do you have a suspect yet?" Liam asked.

"I still need to interview these pets," he replied.

Chirp shot out of the room like his tail was on fire, and Kibbles began her alarm call again. "Woof, woof, woof."

"I don't think that's going to happen." Charlotte sneered. She grabbed her shoes and then picked up Kibbles and walked out of the room.

"Don't forget her sweater. It's tucked into the sleeve of my jacket on the coat tree," Alex said to Charlotte.

Seymour walked over to the fireplace and held his hands up to the warmth of the flames as the dying embers crackled. The detective answered Liam's earlier question, as if Liam had just asked it. "I can't say who the culprit is just yet, but I am enjoying my stay here on your property."

"It's Alex's property now," Liam replied. "Everything that was Nona's is now Alex's."

"And not Charlotte's?" Detective Little questioned.

"She usually used *my* money," Alex replied.

"Aha, a motive." Little shot his finger into the air. "Now we're getting somewhere."

"Motive?" Alex asked, her voice more high pitched than she anticipated. "I don't see how you keep jumping to these bizarre conclusions."

"Now, now, no need to get upset."

"Actually, I'm getting very upset. We have a murderer on the loose. And—"

"The show must go on," Seymour Little interrupted. He perched on the sofa where Charlotte had been.

Liam slid to the edge of his seat. "That brings up another problem we have here. We need a new lead for the play, since Roy can no longer act in that capacity."

"Who's his understudy? That will give us motive for sure," the detective asked, taking off his fedora and placing it on the side table. He brushed his hand over the floral fabrics of the sofa. "Quite nice," he whispered. Then he smoothed out his hair with his fingers and crossed his legs.

Answering his question, Liam replied, "We don't have the budget or staff for understudies. We'll need a stand-in."

He looked to Alex, and she shook her head. "No way! Don't even look at me." Alex tucked the quilt tighter around her legs. "Ask Charlotte."

"I think this is something Nona would want you to do."

"Liam, that's not fair. I'm no actress. I'm supposed to be sleuthing, remember?"

"Will you at least think on it tonight?"

"I will think on it, but I won't do it," Alex replied, and shot to her feet. "I should check on Kibbles. I'll leave you two to plot."

Alex folded the quilt and swung it haphazardly over the back of the chair, then grabbed her shoes before rushing out of the room. At the door, she slid into her shoes and grabbed her jacket, yanking it over her shoulder, leaving the house before both arms were in.

Charlotte walked up the creaky front steps, Kibbles at her heels. "What's wrong?"

"Liam just asked me to star in the play, to replace Roy."

Charlotte erupted in a roaring laugh, causing Kibbles to screech out her alarm call yet again. Alex bent and picked her up. Hugging her close, she soothed the barking pup.

"Let's go back inside, it's freezing out here," Alex said.

"Not freezing. I checked the weather back home. It's twenty degrees warmer here than in Massachusetts. Maybe you need an extra sweater." Charlotte said and followed Alex back inside.

Alex took off her jacket and hung it up. Shaking off the chill, she hugged the wall, hiding from sight of the doorway to the sitting room, and then popped up the stairs two at a time to her guest room.

You guys are on your own!

Kibbles's dog tag clinked against her collar as Charlotte trotted up the steps behind Alex. Charlotte's footfalls were quiet too, and Alex understood Charlotte was avoiding the detective as well.

Kibbles slid into Alex's heels when she stopped short and asked Charlotte, "Your room or mine?"

"Yours, that way it's okay if the pup falls asleep for the night," Charlotte replied, and followed Alex into the room. Chirp tried to sneak through, as Charlotte was closing the door behind herself. "No, sir, you stay out there," Charlotte said, as she shooed the cat back. Successful at her task, she turned and muttered, "That tomcat needs a bell. Sneaky devil."

"I'm glad they are getting along, at least. I can't imagine having to keep them apart so they wouldn't fight all the while we are here."

Alex pulled a hoodie from her bag. She hadn't bothered to unpack or put her clothes in the dresser provided. She'd always preferred to leave her clothes in her travel cases. She tugged the sweatshirt over her head, and her hair fell out of its bun.

"Do you have any idea who Roy's killer might be?" Charlotte asked.

Alex unzipped her accessory bag and fished out her hairbrush. After brushing her long wavy hair, she tied it up into a tight ponytail. "I suspect Emmie, she's acting a bit much. The right hand, left hand . . ."

Charlotte took the brush from Alex and sat. She ran the bristles through her own long golden blonde hair.

"In-con-clu-sive," Charlotte mimicked the detective, and the pair burst out laughing.

Alex kicked off her shoes, and sat on the bed with her legs crossed and a pillow in her lap. "Could be Suzie, myself or Liam," Alex said jokingly.

"It's likely not Wallace, since he passes out at the threat of anxiety. Nor Harrison—he, quote-unquote, saved two people so far." Charlotte pulled her blonde hairs out of the brush, tossed them into the wastebasket and zipped the brush back into Alex's travel bag. "Cute socks, are those otters?"

Alex nodded.

"I think it's Suzie, calling in this actor to portray a *detective*," Charlotte commented. "I'm not sure that *detective* is ever going to figure out who the killer is. Liam is going to have to call the police at some point."

"I can understand why he's reluctant, with the secret society housed here and all."

"Alex, I can't believe you just said that with a straight face," Charlotte teased, and flopped down onto her back, on the bed. "Wait, didn't Suzie say the detective *is* with the local police department."

"Oh, you're right. Ha. We're doomed!" Alex mocked.

Charlotte rolled onto her side and propped herself up on her elbow. "Kinda crazy to be sitting here in the middle of the day, casually discussing which of the people we're spending this week with is a killer!"

"This certainly isn't how I expected my life to play out over the past months. Lawyer, caretaker, victim, adventurer, matriarch, amateur sleuth?"

Charlotte rolled over onto her side, facing Alex, and leaned on her elbow. "You can soon add actor to the list."

"Hilarious! Actually, I suggested *you* take Roy's place in the play."

"What? Why me, and not you?"

"I'm not doing it." Alex slapped her hand on the bed, causing Kibbles to skitter around and then plop at the end of the bed. "That's one thing I'm sure of. I won't do it!"

"So much for a vacation. What did we get ourselves into?"

Alex exhaled a deep sigh. "You mean what did *Nona* get us into, *again*!"

9

A QUILTING STUDIO FIT FOR AN AMBASSADOR

THE NEXT DAY ALEX AWOKE WITH A SMALL FURRY BUM IN her face. "Kibbles, gross." She gently pushed the little bottom away and rolled over. Kibbles's eyes rolled, revealing just the whites of her eyes. "Demon dog, wake up."

Alex rubbed Kibbles's belly and that finally did stir her. "Woof, woof."

"What do you mean, no?" Alex scratched the pooch's back. "No doubt we have another eventful day ahead of us?"

Alex rolled out of bed and checked the window. *No one lurking out there.*

She turned back to her furry companion, "I had the strangest dream. And I had an inspiration for the speech."

Kibbles hopped up and down on the bed. "Woof."

Alex found a pen and a scrap of paper in her bag and jotted down a couple notes. "Good, I'm glad you want to hear about it." Alex carried her toiletry bag to the en suite bathroom and pulled out her toothbrush and toothpaste. "I was going to tell you, regardless."

Kibbles quirked one eyebrow. "Woof."

"Let's go, we need to brush *your* teeth too."

A double bark of protest, and Kibbles covered her face with her paws.

"Okay, you can have a pass, since we're technically on vacation." Alex turned back to the bathroom.

"Woo-oof!"

"I dreamt Nona was here in Mishap."

Kibbles barked twice again, while Alex finished brushing her teeth and then rinsed her mouth. "No, I know she's not really here, though she is in *spirit*. It was like a vision." Alex wiped her face on the hand towel and wrapped her ponytail into a bun, then secured it with an elastic.

"It was really a nightmare, because Nona said I must perform in the play. That it'll help us solve Roy's murder."

"Woof, woof, woof." Kibbles ran to the end of the bed and stared at Alex, who then picked up her canine companion and hugged her. Little black and tan strands of fur covered the front of Alex's dark gray sweatshirt. "You have bed head, silly." Alex brushed the dog's fur with her fingers and scratched under Kibbles's chin. "Don't worry, we won't be in any danger." She set the dog back down on the bed. "I hope."

I'll do it, but only if Charlotte helps.

Alex changed her clothes, and she and Kibbles trotted downstairs to the breakfast room. Charlotte was already seated, picking at a piece of toast. A tall pitcher of peach juice obscured her mischievous grin until Alex sat beside her.

What's she been up to this morning?

"You just missed the good detective, Alex."

That explains it.

"Good morning, Liam," Alex greeted the elderly man, who was dressed in a tweed blazer with elbow patches. *I didn't know people still wore that kind of jacket.*

"I hope you both had a fine sleep."

"Woof."

"Yes. It was good to get some extra z's. Although, I'm sure you meant Charlotte and me, but Kibbles did as well." Alex chuckled. "I've decided, I will help you with the play—against my better judgment." She picked up the pitcher of peach juice and a glass and poured herself a full cup. "But only if Charlotte helps too."

Charlotte mouthed the word 'no,' then popped the last piece of her toast into her mouth.

Alex mouthed the word 'yes' and guzzled her juice.

Later that morning, Liam led Alex, Charlotte and Kibbles through the maze of hallways and rooms in the back of the theater to the quilt studio.

Ha, Charlotte didn't even know she was walking right by the studio. At least half a dozen times.

Charlotte flashed a bemused expression at Liam, their reserved steward.

Liam pulled out a large key ring, selected the right key and unlocked the inconspicuous door.

This should assuage Charlotte's insistence.

Alex crossed her fingers behind her back as Kibbles jumped at her leg, trying to get up. "Walk, baby. Use your legs, you have four of them."

Charlotte vibrated with anticipation, her hands literally trembling.

"Why do you lock it?"

"You'll see," Liam responded, and flashed Alex an apologetic smile before reaching around the door to flip the lights on.

"Wow!" Charlotte squealed.

Kibble ran in circles.

"It's okay, Kibbs, she's happy. No cause for alarm." Alex picked up the crazed dog before stepping through the door into a quilting studio *to die for*. "Holy mackerel!"

"Wooof!" Kibbles echoed her statement.

Charlotte's eyes were bulging. "The room must run the length of the building.".

No creaky wooden floorboards—instead, pristine white concrete covered the expanse. Bookshelves lined the walls, ready for fabric and supplies. The studio was as bright as a dentist office in contrast to the dark ambiance of the theater rooms and halls.

A dozen magazine-worthy workstations were set in two rows of six. Each with a brand-new sewing machine.

"Nona set this up?" Alex asked. "She's never even used a sewing machine. How?"

Charlotte ran her hand along one of the tables set up with cutting mats, rulers, rotary cutters and every other imaginable quilting and sewing accessory and notion needed.

"Well, yes, she set this up, so to speak."

Alex sat, with Kibbles in her lap, in one of the sewing-themed, ergonomic chairs perched at each table, and spun around like a child. Kibbles jumped off mid spin.

Liam grinned from ear to ear, "But—"

"Here it comes," Alex grumbled as her excitement waned. "But what?"

"Well, there's a bit of a hitch. I'm not quite sure how Nona planned to resolve the quandary."

Charlotte's gleeful expression faltered. "Of—"

Liam gestured to the expanse of tables. "She contracted with this sewing machine company, to be a spokesperson."

"You mean a brand ambassador? Nona? For a sewing machine company?" Charlotte cackled and doubled over with hysteria.

"I've heard stranger things," Alex said. "No, wait. I haven't," she quipped, and laughed. Kibbles ran in circles until Alex held out her hands for the dog, who jumped back into her lap and licked her face. "Shh, it's okay, baby."

"I received a notice that she didn't fulfill her obligations as the *ambassador*, so you call it, and the company would like us to send back all the machines, or pay for them."

"Nooo," Charlotte exclaimed.

Alex peered around the room. "I'll pay. It's fine."

Charlotte flicked her eyes between Liam and Alex. "Alex can be the ambassador."

"Say what? No. I will not. That's too much to ask."

"I've told them all about both of you. You can choose who. Here's the phone number." Liam gave both Alex and Charlotte a business card for the Sewlock Sewing Machine Company.

"What did you get us into, Liam? You're just as bad as Nona." Alex flashed him a teasing glance. She reviewed the business card. "The same company the cruise lines used."

Liam leaned back against the table and said, "It would be such a shame to see these machines go back and the actors never learn to quilt."

"Oh, stop." Alex waved her hand and shook her head. "That schtick isn't going to work on me."

Charlotte turned in circles, gazing at the entire space. "I'll do it," she agreed. "I'll teach the cast to quilt, and I'll be the brand ambassador, so we can keep all this."

"Wonderful!" Liam clapped, "I'm sure you'll find it very rewarding."

Alex fiddled with a cup full of marking pens and pencils.

"This studio has everything!" Charlotte whooped.

"Are you sure, you want to take all this on, Charlotte? You don't even know what Nona agreed to."

Charlotte walked the perimeter of the room as if plotting out how to finish the studio. "How bad could it be?"

Alex shot her a warning look. "This is Nona we're talking about!"

The afternoon came quickly after the big quilting studio reveal. Backstage, Alex was wearing a dress that looked like it was circa the 1800s. "I can't believe the star role was a Southern belle, and they had Roy playing the part." Standing on a crate, Alex dipped her head to catch a glimpse of Charlotte below, just as a pin poked her in the ankle. "Ouch."

"Be still, Alex."

"Well, stop *pinning* me, then." Alex jerked her leg away from Charlotte's advance with the pincushion.

"I'll poke you too, now stop fidgeting." Charlotte's bellowing laugh echoed through the empty backstage area.

Where is everyone?

"Alex, are you trying to say a man can't play the role of the leading lady?"

"No, not at all. I was just thinking he was over six feet tall. And I am smaller in every way possible, and let's leave it that." Alex laughed. *I'm a respectable five foot—*

Her thoughts were interrupted by none other than the detective.

"Detective Little. Have you come to share news that you've caught the murderer?" Charlotte squawked, antagonizing him before Alex had the chance to greet him.

Alex studied his face. Something was off about his wrinkles. *I don't think he's actually as old as he* looks. "Ouch, Charlotte, easy! Don't you know how to use those things?"

"Quilter. Remember. Not a seamstress." Charlotte held the pincushion up mockingly, like a prize she'd won.

She knows how to use pins, there's no fooling me. She's poking me on purpose, brat.

The two friends bantering like teenagers, however, was working toward breaking down the wall Alex had put up after their most recent fight.

Little reinserted himself into the conversation. "I was quite the actor in my day, you know. I was in the play *Man of La Mancha.*"

"Oh really, did you play Don Quixote?" Charlotte asked.

"No, I played Dapple." The detective straightened with an air of pride.

"Wasn't that the donkey?" Charlotte asked in a deadpan tone.

Alex stifled a laugh, covering her mouth with her hand.

"Okay, that should do it. Come off your pedestal, Alex. Give us a twirl. Easy, though, you don't want to poke yourself with a pin."

"*A* pin? Really? No one here is going to stitch the hem? I'm supposed to deliver my lines flawlessly, while simultaneously trying not to be stabbed by a thousand pins?" Alex eyed the near empty pincushion, which was the size of a dessert plate.

"Look at all this lace"—Charlotte made a disgusted face—

"and frilly stuff. I suppose we could try to hand stitch it, but it would take all day."

Alex shrugged. *Right now I'd much rather be sewing than learning lines and starring in a play.*

Alex swirled the dress around and only poked herself three times in doing so.

"Let's try your lines again." Charlotte changed tack. "We need the spotlight so you can truly experience what it will be like."

The spotlight lit up Alex on cue.

A sultry voice sang out of the darkness. "*Happy Birthday, Detective Seymour.*"

"I can't keep my lines straight with Marilyn singing like that." Alex wiped sweat from her brow. "I'm sweating in this gown." Alex scratched her shoulder. "This thing is as itchy as—"

Charlotte put her index finger to her own lips. "Your lines, Alex. You need to memorize them. How do you think Uncle Sam feels? His hat weighs like twenty pounds! I don't know what Roy was thinking when he designed these costumes."

"You can't be serious about the lines."

"Hey, don't shoot the messenger, I didn't write the play. How hard can it be to memorize the opening lines from the Gettysburg address and introduce the actors?" Charlotte asked.

"Fine! Seven score and four months ago. There was a man—"

"Wow, you really are bad at this. You've delivered the line wrong."

"This whole thing is backward. How's anyone to figure out what all these characters have in common?"

"It's all in the delivery of the lines." Charlotte picked up a manuscript from a nearby stool and shoved it at Alex. "Didn't you have to *act* in front of judges while you were lawyering in New York?"

"No. That wasn't acting, that was serious. Real life. People's lives were at stake."

Well, at least I thought it was. Now I don't really know what was real or staged!

Charlotte stood in front of her, perfectly poised for the role, her arms in just the right position. "Here. Hold your arms out and poise your fingers like this."

Alex mimicked Charlotte's stance, dropping the manuscript.

"No, Alex, you're too stiff. Like this." Charlotte molded Alex's hand, curving her fingers into place.

Charlotte was graceful in ways Alex would never be, and she'd already memorized all the lines to help Alex learn them. "You do it, Charlotte. You're clearly made for this role. Complete with the golden locks." Alex twirled a tendril of cocoa-colored hair that had fallen loose from beneath her silver blonde wig.

"You think so?" Charlotte feigned humility.

"We're the same size. You know the lines. Why don't you take over the part?"

Charlotte picked up the manuscript and held it to her chest. Her eyes were gleaming, and her cheeks were flushed. "Are you sure?"

"I still have to speak at the unveiling ceremony tomorrow, so, ah, yes. I'm as sure about you performing the part as I am sure I don't want to do it. This is your moment to shine. What can go wrong?"

10

A DEDICATION AND A SURPRISE

The remainder of the previous evening had flowed without a hitch. No signs of impending danger, no further sightings of the blasted detective, and Alex had successfully wriggled out of the lead role in the play—which she'd never wanted to perform in to begin with.

Alex awoke refreshed but the window panes shook, signaling another bitter winter day in Georgia. She bundled up to face the cold, though her spirits were higher than the day before. Outside in the courtyard, something shiny caught her eye. Alex noticed a single red Christmas ornament hanging from a bare branch of a potted tree. She walked the grounds with Kibbles and met up with Charlotte.

Alex shivered in her coat as she and Charlotte stood by the banner for the Gretta Galia Memorial Theater. Alex's heart was hammering in her chest. She surveyed the outdoor setup, a small stage perched in the center of the large, square courtyard between the house and the theater. Rows of folding chairs were staggered, facing the makeshift platform. The animals were as mischievous as ever—Kibbles skittering around chasing Chirp, and Chirp darting between the chairs. Alex couldn't help but smile at the small dog's wagging black tail with tan skunk stripe. The feline had quickly established himself as a friend to Kibbles, but Alex couldn't deny her own affection for the spunky tomcat.

Detective Little stood off to the side, eyeing the guests as they arrived, found their seats and held onto their hats. The wind picked up just as the ceremony started. The program boasted a welcome from Liam, the reading of a poem, a short comedy skit and even a special video created by the actors as a tribute to their benefactor—Nona.

Finally, Liam introduced Alex and Charlotte, and they made their way toward the stage. Alex pulled back her fur-lined hood and was grateful she opted for a tight bun and not a messy one, as the wind threatened to make a mockery of her hairdo. She took her place at the podium, shivering slightly as she spoke.

I said I wasn't going to give any speeches, and here I am.

"Thank you all for coming today." Her voice was barely audible over the howling wind. She cleared her throat and spoke louder. "We are here to honor our grandmother, who was a true believer in students of all ages."

Alex continued, hoping her words would warm the hearts of the small audience, despite the chill in the air. "Nona was a woman who believed in the power to inspire, educate, and entertain. It was her mission to create safe places where students and artists could learn unencumbered by the pressures of financial burdens. It's my hope this theater will continue to carry on her legacy for many generations to come." Smiling, the audience applauded as Alex stepped away from the podium.

"That was great, Alex. Where'd you come up with that?" Charlotte whispered.

"I don't know. It just came to me last night."

Together, they picked up the giant scissors and held them

up to the enormous gold bow for the obligatory photo op. They paused while cameras flashed like mad, and then they cut the ribbon.

Pride and satisfaction washed over Alex, and they made their way off the stage. Kibbles trotted alongside her, tail wagging. "Woof."

"Thank you, my furry friend," Alex whispered just before Kibbles scampered off after Chirp again. With Kibbles's superior intellect and rigid training, Alex had no fear of the dog running off, getting lost, or even leaving the courtyard—as long as Chirp didn't.

Nona would have loved this. The sharp pain of regret filled her heart.

Before the ceremony was complete, Liam approached the tarp-covered statue. "Ladies and gentlemen, may I have your attention for a few more moments. I have one more surprise, then we can head in for refreshments."

The onlookers all turned their heads in his direction, toward the center of the courtyard, and Liam tugged on a cord holding the tarp. The covering came off, revealing a life-size statue of none other than—Nona herself. A marble version, of course. She stood, poised in a pants suit, with a quilt in one hand and a sewing needle in the other. The audience sprang to their feet in a thundering round of applause. Once the attention died down, the guests dispersed, moving out of the frigid air and into the theater.

Glasses of sparkling cider lined every appropriate flat surface, and Liam was in his glory, showing off the opulent updated interior.

"Well, we made it through without incident," Charlotte commented, grabbing a champagne flute of the nonalcoholic bubbly. "I'll need something stronger than this later." She winked at Alex.

"I think you spoke too soon." Alex pointed toward the ceiling.

"Chirp!" Charlotte shrieked. The cat was tightrope walking across the top of the stage curtain. "That cat is always up to no good."

After the ceremony, and before the play, Alex had just enough time to coax Kibbles into the travel crate. Chirp wasn't in sight, but he was Liam's problem. She quickly changed into an evening gown and headed straight for the theater to help Charlotte—the star of the play.

Alex entered the building through the back, and peeked out into the audience. The theater was packed. She heaved a sigh of relief that the hard part was nearly over.

You realize you're comparing a theater play as the hard part versus solving the mystery of Roy's murder—which we aren't any closer to resolving.

The audience held a collective breath as the curtains parted to reveal the grand stage. The spotlight illuminated a stunning young woman dressed in a period gown with a voluminous skirt adorned with too much lace and frills.Charlotte, the Southern belle, was about to deliver a pivotal monologue for the play. She took a deep breath as she prepared to speak her lines. Her first line rang out loud and clear across the theater, and Alex smiled, happy for her best friend's success.

But Alex's senses were on high alert, so for her, Charlotte's elation was quickly overshadowed by a commotion backstage as a weighted bag used for set decoration was hurtling toward Charlotte's head—and Charlotte had no idea what was about to happen. She continued to articulate her lines, her voice clear and unwavering, even as the bag descended on a direct path to hitting her.

Alex sprinted toward Charlotte, her eyes fixed on the weighted bag. The audience gasped in shock at her sudden appearance. With lightning-fast reflexes, Alex pushed a tree prop across the stage; the weighted bag hit the wooden prop and deflected, narrowly missing Charlotte. A collective sigh of relief burst across the guests as the bag thudded onto the stage floor behind Charlotte. With the crowd staring, Alex gave a curtsy and strode into the darkness of backstage to keep watching.

Charlotte paused for a moment, unaware of what had just happened, and then kept going. With a shaky breath, she continued her last lines. Without introducing the next act, Charlotte bowed. The audience's applause was thunderous, and Charlotte took one more deep bow and heaved a huge sigh.

As the curtains closed, Charlotte turned toward Alex, eyes wide. Beside Alex, Detective Little stood unmoving, still gawking after Alex's quick thinking, which had saved Charlotte's life. When Charlotte exited the stage, she asked, "Oh my goodness, Alex, what was that all about?"

"Someone just tried to kill you, Charlotte. And now I'm more determined than ever to get to the bottom of this and solve this case."

"Or someone tried to kill *you*, Alex," Seymour contradicted her. He pulled out his notepad and scribbled something with a golf pencil.

"Why me?" Alex asked. "The bag was clearly aimed to hit Charlotte."

"Because *you* were the one who was supposed to be delivering the lines tonight."

For the first time since they'd met Detective Seymour Little, one of his theories actually had merit.

"Who else knew you two had switched places?" the detective asked.

"You." Alex pointed to the detective. The crowd erupted in a volley of applause behind them as they skirted off the stage just before the curtain opened for the next segment of the play. Uncle Sam rushed by as Charlotte and Alex returned to the backstage area.

"Alex and I." Charlotte added, "Liam, Emmie . . . and Dave. But I know it wasn't Dave!"

"Who's Dave?" Alex and the detective asked simultaneously.

Suzie rushed up. "Charlotte, I need your help with my costume, please hurry! I'm about to go on!"

Charlotte glanced over her shoulder with a grin as Suzie dragged her away. "We'll talk later!"

11

INVESTIGATIONS

CHARLOTTE DRAGGED ALEX ONTO THE STAGE FOR THE curtain call. All the actors took their bows. And the audience rose to their feet, throwing flowers for a standing ovation.

Despite the near miss, the play was an instant success—delivered to an eager audience without another hitch.

Liam handed Charlotte a bouquet of pink and white roses, and the line of actors stepped back, allowing Charlotte to shine in the spotlight.

Backstage a few minutes later, Alex set her mind to finding the culprit. "We have to question everyone again. Find out where they were all day."

"I examined the rope. It was cut, or maybe slashed, with a saw or some other type of tool," Little added.

What kind of tool? Alex looked around.

"A broken winch?" Charlotte wondered aloud.

Liam appeared with a hot tea and handed it to Charlotte. "Are you okay?"

"Yes, of course." She sipped the tea. "Thank you. We were just discussing the rope and what tool may have caused it to break, or be cut."

"Broken winch?" Liam suggested.

"That was Charlotte's thought as well. That might imply it was just an accident after all," Alex suggested. She surveyed the complicated web of wires, lighting, and rigging directly above.

A serious look crossed Liam's face. "I'll have Dave, the handyman, look into it right away."

"Unless he's the someone who meant for it to drop on Charlotte, or me, in the first place." Alex suggested.

Charlotte eyed Alex with a concerned expression, her brows knitted. "Not Dave! What would be his motive?"

"I don't know who or why, but we need to find out soon, before something else happens," Alex replied.

Charlotte wriggled out of her costume, and Alex reached up to help with the dress, revealing a full-body leotard underneath. "It's not like we were closing in on Roy's murderer or anything. I know we were planning on leaving this weekend, but maybe we should stay longer. After all, we don't want to leave Liam here with a murderer on the loose."

"As much as I'd love to stay, I need to get back to Spruce Street." Alex grimaced.

"What's the rush? I'm in no hurry to get back."

"I need to get back to Salem. I had hoped the DNA results from the knife that we found would've been back already. Or the fingerprints, even."

"Maybe Liam will have knowledge or clues to help, but meanwhile we need to solve *this* case first."

"Yes, that's exactly what I was suggesting, Captain Obvious." Alex chuckled.

"Oh-kay, I don't recall you saying anything of the sort, brat!" Charlotte stuck out her tongue like she was twelve.

"Well, I have to worry about everything, all at the same time. Just because I'm here, doesn't mean I'm not still thinking about the problems we left behind back home, and vice versa."

Charlotte turned away but said, "I haven't forgotten either, Alex."

Detective Little stopped pacing. "We should start right after breakfast in the morning?"

"And there *he* is again," Charlotte mumbled.

"No. We start now," Alex insisted. "The play is over and all the actors are still here."

The detective removed his fedora and scratched his head. "But it's late. I'm tired, and my feet hurt."

"What'd he just say?" Charlotte's face flushed with anger. "Those would be my feet, if anyone's feet hurt." Charlotte reached down to loosen the strap of one of her heels, and Alex caught her hand, and the shoe, as they came up too quickly in Detective Little's direction.

"Alex, he's not even wearing dress shoes." Alex eyed the detective's sneakers. "Are you even a real detective?" Charlotte snarled.

"Of course, I just wasn't prepared for a fancy event when you called on me to come solve this case."

Alex resisted tossing Charlotte's high heel at him herself. Instead, she pulled Charlotte away. "We'll have Emmie get you some coffee. Let's go."

Backstage, amongst the celebrating actors, clinking champagne flutes, high fives and animated congratulations, a dark cloud still hung over the event, and Alex was determined to uncover Roy's killer.

Alex cleared her throat. "I hate to break up the celebration, but we can't delay solving Roy's murder any longer."

The troupe of actors pooh-poohed her interruption.

"We're going to need to question you all again."

"Awww, buzz*kill*," the actress dressed as Marilyn Monroe said, and the actor dressed as Uncle Sam flashed her a grimace. "What? Too soon?" she replied to his grimace.

"Yes, Jojo, too soon." He said, as if his look wasn't enough to answer her back.

"No one liked Roy anyways," Jojo replied, removing her blonde wig and revealing her long, curly red hair.

Suzie hooked her arm around her uncle's. "I liked Roy. Don't speak ill of the dead."

"Do we really have to do this now? Can't it wait until the morning?" Uncle Sam said, taking off his top hat. "This hat weighs a ton. My back is *killing* me."

"Too soon Norman," Jojo said in a singsong voice.

"You didn't have to wear *this*," Emmie complained, holding up her hat, which had a bag of cash erupting from the top.

"Or those," Dave replied, prodding Norman to hold up his platform shoes that he wore with his Uncle Sam costume.

"Right. Liam was about to fetch you, Dave. Let's start with you," Alex said.

"Me? Why me? I didn't do anything! I wasn't even here when Roy was—"

Alex turned to Emmie, who'd tucked her cash hat under her arm. "Can you get us some coffee, please? Add a shot of caffeine for my detective friend here."

Emmie threw the money hat on the ground and stormed off.

"Watch out for that one," the detective responded. He stood off to the side, unconcerned by Alex's appropriation of the investigation.

Alex showed Dave to a seat. "Have a seat, Mr.—"

"Dave, just Dave," he replied in a squeaky voice.

"I'm afraid I'll need your full name, please," Detective Little insisted, sitting beside Alex. He pulled out his notepad.

"Dave Dillard." He said and tipped his head.

The detective scratched the name down.

Charlotte sat on the other side of Alex. She was free of her Southern belle costume and now her stage makeup. In her jeans and a baggy sweatshirt, like Alex wished she herself were—opposed to her silk evening gown. Charlotte had set out another of Liam's elaborate charcuterie boards, this one triple the size of the previous one—large enough to feed several troupes. A pepperoni rose was centered within half a dozen different types of crackers and twice as many varieties of cheese. Fresh fruits lined the perimeter.

Where'd she get that?

"You said you were not here when Roy was murdered. That doesn't absolve you. Where *were* you?" Alex asked in a serious tone.

A dim yellow light shone over Dave's balding head as he answered, "I was at home, tending to my sick mother."

"What's your role here with the theater?" Alex asked.

Emmie arrived with a pot of coffee, disposable cups and plastic spoons on a wooden tray, along with cream and sugar.

Charlotte made herself a cheese-and-cracker sandwich, and Alex's stomach growled.

"I guess you could say I'm a jack-of-all-trades. I do a bit of carpentry, handiwork, janitorial, whatever Liam needs done."

"Like having someone murdered?" the detective asked.

Dave's face paled, and he rubbed his hands on his pant legs. "No! Say what? No! You think Liam wanted Roy killed and hired me to do it? You're mad!"

Alex looked at Detective Little in disbelief. *What the heck is this guy doing?*

"The deceased was found in the janitor's closet. That would technically be your domain, would it not?"

"I'm not dumb enough to kill someone, and then leave them in a place associated with my work!" Dave protested.

"Well, it would either make you the most likely suspect, or the worst," Little commented.

Liam entered the warehouse-turned-dressing-room, turned-interrogation-space. He nodded to Dave, then flashed a perplexed look at Alex. "What's wrong?"

Charlotte popped a grape into her mouth. "Pull up a seat, Liam. The show is just getting started!"

"So, Dave, why would you want to kill Charlotte?" the detective continued.

"I wouldn't, I didn't," Dave stuttered. "I *like* Charlotte." His face flushed red.

Charlotte made herself another cracker sandwich and crunched on it.

Dave's eyes widened, and a smile formed at the corner of his lips. "She's the star of the show."

I think Dave's smitten with Charlotte.

Seymour put his cupped hand to his ear. "What did he say?"

"You're sitting right here. How did you not hear him?" Charlotte spoke loudly. "I think you should check your hearing aid."

I don't think he wears one.

"Never mind. That's all for now, Dave. You may go." The detective shooed him away with one hand.

"You're up next, Wallace." Liam waved for Wallace to take a seat with Alex, the detective and Charlotte.

"Who's this guy?" Charlotte whispered, flicking a judgmental glance in his direction.

"When we found Roy, remember. He's the one who has the fainting condition," Alex whispered back.

Charlotte's head was down, her attention focused on her cell phone. "Then he can't be the killer."

Wallace sat down and dropped his dog's head mask on the floor beside his chair.

"So, Ace, did you kill Roy?" the detective asked abruptly.

"What? No. He was my best friend, why would I kill him? And my name's Wallace, not Ace."

"Fine, you can go now." Little dismissed him.

Alex blinked. "What? That's it?"

Suddenly Charlotte screamed and held up her clenched hand. She stood up, and thick red liquid was dripping from her palm. Alex jumped to her feet, and Charlotte whispered, "Cherry."

Alex glanced back at their interviewee, Wallace, who had turned ghostly white. He swayed in his seat, and then he slumped, his head hitting the table.

"Oh crap, I thought he was faking it." Charlotte grimaced. She opened her hand and held out the squished cherry, showing the cherry juice staining her fingers. "Is he all right?"

Detective Little fanned Wallace with his notepad.

Wallace came to. Charlotte quickly showed him it was just cherry juice, not blood.

"I think it is safe to rule him out due to his *condition*," Little noted.

"He kinda had that 'always a bridesmaid, never a bride' vibe. Don't you think?" Charlotte asked, wiping her hands off on a rag she'd found on one of the warehouse shelves.

Huh?

"The murder of Roy would certainly have triggered the emotional distress enough to cause him to faint," Alex responded. "If he had, he would've fallen right into the blood pool in the closet, but it wasn't disturbed."

Detective Little stood. "Excuse me, ladies, but I'm in need of a short respite, as I'm sure you are as well. Why don't we break for a little while, and then reconvene here to conduct the remainder of the interviews?"

Alex and Charlotte agreed, and the detective walked away abruptly, behind Wallace.

As they left the theater, Alex glanced around nervously. The courtyard seemed more ominous than it had in the past few days, like someone might be lurking in the shadows. A sneaking suspicion hit her that she had no idea what was really going on here in Mishap, with the murder and the stage accident. A feeling that would stay with her long after the final curtain call.

12

PULL UP A SEAT AND GRAB SOME POPCORN

Back in the main house, Charlotte was sitting in the library, busy with her phone, and Alex sat across the small table from her in the black leather armchair. "I've found some good and bad press about the play. Which do you want first?"

"On social media?" Alex asked, and Charlotte nodded. "Give us the good first. I'm sure it's all about you."

"'Up and Coming New Star, Charlotte Galia,' 'Gorgeous Southern Belle Makes Her Debut,' 'A Star is Born.'"

"Wow, that's great! You were awesome." Alex winked. "I'd say clip those headlines, but, you know, social media and all."

"There is one about you too, Alex."

"Really? What's it say?"

"'Lady in Black Satin Saves Star of the Show,'" Charlotte replied.

"Hmm, I guess that's good. They didn't mention my name, did they?"

Charlotte swept her hair up into a ponytail. "No."

"Okay, well, let's save that for later. We need to solve this case. Quickly, preferably in the next forty-eight hours, so we're not delayed in going home."

"Fine, the bad, then?" Charlotte didn't wait for Alex to respond, and blurted out the bad headlines, rapid-fire, scrolling as she said them. "'The Play Was Doomed from the Start,' 'No One Could Get Their Act Together,' 'I Thought the Play Was Going to Be About Quilting.'"

"You would think so!" Alex chuckled.

"And my personal favorite," Charlotte added, "'Third Time Was Not a Charm(er).'"

"Those are awful! Who wrote that last one?" Alex asked.

"I'm not sure, they're all from the same account: Cheddar Chatter. Not a very inspired choice." Charlotte looked up from the phone and picked a strawberry from the bowl in the center of the table. "Who do you think that is?"

"Well, it has to be one of the actors. Who else would know there were potentially three leading *ladies*, so to speak?" Alex pursed her lips. "Sounds like Emmie to me, though I'll have to puzzle it out."

"I think we should save her for last."

Alex sat forward on the edge of her seat. "I've had a bad feeling about her this whole time. She's definitely disgruntled about something. And working against the detective, for sure."

Charlotte relaxed against the back of the suede armchair, with another berry. "Probably because she's Liam's *right-hand* woman," Charlotte cackled. "And all she does is get coffee."

"I see what you did there, clever. Or, it might be because of that crazy costume. Couldn't they have come up with a better way to represent money?" Alex questioned. "The fact Nona had anything to do with this play might just make sense." Alex gazed down and tapped the program that was laying on the table, getting Charlotte's attention.

Man's Best Friend - Screenplay written by Suzie Que and Nona Galia.

"I would've thought it would be about quilting in some way? Though, I can't wait to see the headlines in the local newspaper." Charlotte beamed. "*Those* ones I can clip."

"You were brilliant, my friend. A superstar! But let's get back to the theater to interview the next person, shall we?"

"What about the detective? Should we wait for him before continuing?"

"Really, Charlotte, I thought you had a distaste for our friend, the good detective."

Charlotte set her phone on the table and looked through the program booklet, her eyes alight with amusement. "I don't care for him one bit, or his bumbling act either."

Alex ate a couple of strawberries. She turned to Charlotte and smiled, showing her teeth.

"Nope, nothing in your teeth. Mine?" Charlotte asked, and smiled back at Alex, showing her teeth as well.

"Nope, you're good. Let's head back to the theater."

Alex and Charlotte bundled back up and walked across the courtyard to the theater.

Inside, they settled again backstage around an eight-foot folding table where they'd conducted the first few interviews. Liam set down a few bottles of water, and Alex swigged more than half of one before saying, "Liam, let's interview Marilyn, ah, Jojo, next."

"Of course. I'll get us fresh coffee as well."

Alex rubbed the chill from her arms. "Liam, is there any hot chocolate?"

Liam answered Alex, "Yes, I'll have Emmie get us both." The detective sat down to join the interrogations again.

"Detective! *Happy Birthday, Detective,*" Jojo sang, in full costume, ignoring his stern expression.

Why did she put her wig back on, that's odd.

The detective blushed. "That's very impressive, Marilyn, I mean Jojo. But we really need to ask you some questions about Roy's murder."

"Of course. What do you need to know?"

"Did Roy have any enemies?" Little asked.

"Only everyone he ever made a costume for. Except me, of

course." She looked down at her sheer dress and smiled appreciatively. "He might've known how to hem a dress, but he was a terrible *costume* designer."

"Did you have a relationship with Roy?" Alex asked.

"No, certainly not," Jojo replied, one eyebrow raised skeptically. "I'm married to my work."

"Are you certain you were not *with* Roy?"

The questioning went no where with Jojo, and while they hadn't received any clues that would help determine exactly *who* had killed Roy, they did discover a new motive—a cast of actors who were unhappy with the costumes he'd made.

A few minutes later, Charlotte had vanished and Liam was looking for Emmie. Alex and Detective Little were sitting across from Norman, the actor playing Uncle Sam.

Little started, "So . . ." But before the detective could ask him any questions, Norman interrupted, launching into a rant about his costume.

"Can we talk about this?" He pointed to his hat. "I mean, how am I supposed to perform in this thing? It's way too heavy," Norman said, frustration evident in his voice.

The detective exchanged a glance with Alex, who was equally surprised by the sudden outburst.

"And the inseams are never right," Norman complained.

"I understand the costume is uncomfortable," Alex replied. "But we need to talk about Roy's murder. Are you upset enough to have killed him?"

"No, of course not. I'm a professional," Norman replied, his nose wrinkled in disgust, his frustration with the costume evidently forgotten. He sighed, running a hand through his hair. "I just want to get out of this darn outfit."

"Okay, that's it for now." Detective Little dismissed the man and his top hat.

"Wait." Alex said, before Norman had even stood up all the

way. She sat forward. "I have more questions. Did you want to play the lead?"

"No way, I'd never fit in that Southern belle dress," Norman replied and scratched his head.

"Why did you take a picture of Roy's dead body?" Alex asked.

"I'm sorry, I wasn't trying to be disrespectful. I belong to a club of amateur sleuths." He flashed an apologetic look to Alex.

Little tapped his notepad, but didn't write anything in it. "Okay, you may go."

Norman nodded, standing up. "Thanks," he said, fidgeting with the heavy ensemble. "I'm glad this play is behind us. Hopefully, we'll have hired a new designer before the next one begins."

As he hurried off, Alex checked off 'motive' on a mental list she'd been keeping of who was unhappy with their costumes.

The interrogation continued as Alex and Detective Little probed for more information and tried to piece together the truth behind everyone's whereabouts on the day in question.

Where's Charlotte?

Harrison sat across from Alex, his shoulders square and his back stiff. Alex rubbed her own shoulder and studied him for a moment. Detective Little asked, "Can you tell us a little bit about your role on the set?"

Harrison relaxed at this question. "Sure. I'm in charge of all the lighting and sound equipment. I oversee the set up and operation of all the equipment used during the play."

"Sounds like an important job," Little said with a coy smile.

"Yeah, I guess so."

"Harrison, can you tell us where you were when the murder occurred?"

"I was at the control board."

"Did anything unusual happen after breakfast?" Alex asked.

"I saw Emmie, she was muttering to herself. She seemed to be in a rush to get somewhere, but I don't know where she disappeared to. I didn't see her after that."

"Okay. Thank you." The detective scratched notes in his pad. "Let me ask you this, did you or any of the other actors have a conflict with the victim, either personally or professionally?"

Harrison hesitated, then let out a sigh. "Okay, fine. The truth is, we had a disagreement about the sound design for the show. He wanted something different than what I had planned, but it wasn't his call. We had a bit of a heated argument about it. He should've stayed in his lane." Harrison scoffed, "I didn't bust him up about his terrible costumes."

Little leaned back in his chair, taking in the information. "And what was the outcome of that argument?"

Harrison shrugged. "We agreed to disagree."

The detective nodded, jotting down notes. "Thank you, Harrison."

The clock struck midnight as they finished interviewing Harrison, saving Suzie and Emmie, Alex's two most likely suspects, for last.

Alex's stomach rumbled, and she popped a cheese cube into her mouth and chewed inconspicuously wondering where Charlotte had gone off to. She and the detective sat across the table from his niece, Suzie.

"Can you tell me what you were doing the day of the murder?" Little's voice was steady and calming.

"I was backstage, transforming into my character. I've never played a cat before."

"You were great, just great!" he replied.

Alex cleared her throat, and Little's face hardened. "Do you have any idea who might have committed the murder?" he asked.

Suzie shook her head. "I didn't see Roy after breakfast. We all had coffee and muffins in the mezzanine. It wasn't until the afternoon when I did a fitting with my costume that I realized I needed Roy to hem my pants. I looked all over for him. Well, not all over, because I didn't think to check the janitor's closet. I never go in there. No need."

"Of course, dear, no need to trouble yourself with janitorial supplies."

Alex scoffed and asked, "Did you see Emmie after breakfast?"

"No, not that I recall. I thought she was with Liam. For your arrival, I mean."

Alex flashed her a polite smile and responded, "Yes, she was."

"Okay, Suzie Que," Seymour said, standing up from the table. "That's all for now."

She nodded and stood also, looking relieved.

"Wait just a minute," Alex demanded. The relief on Suzie's face diminished. "Did you audition for the lead role in the play?"

"No, I specifically requested the cat part as sort of a personal and professional challenge."

The detective beamed with pride for his niece.

Suzie added, "No one wanted to be the Southern belle, that's why Roy got stuck with it."

A play where no one wants to be the lead? Alex pondered.

Little scratched something off in his notebook and said, "I may need to speak with you again if I have any further questions."

"Of course, Uncle. Anything to help you with the investigation," Suzie said before leaving.

The detective excused himself again, "I'll take a short break."

Charlotte appeared and took a seat next to Alex.

"Where have you been?" Alex questioned her friend.

Charlotte held up a popcorn bag and nodded toward it.

Alex chuckled, "Did you go all the way to Massachusetts to get it?"

Alex tapped her finger on the table waiting anxiously for the detective to return, while Charlotte sat beside her, munching from the bag of popcorn.

She had to be doing more than just getting popcorn. Alex rolled up a slice of pepperoni around a cheese cube just before her stomach let out a loud groan.

"Chirp showed me the secret passageway." Charlotte replied and waggled her eyebrows.

"You'll have to show me tomorrow." Alex said staring past Charlotte. She hadn't spotted it before, but the props on the shelves cast ominous shadows across the walls. *Spooky. We need to get on with this.*

"Are we getting on with this interview or not." Emmie scoffed.

Where's that detective? Is he sweating his suspect?

Alex checked her watch. Ten minutes had gone by. *The actors must need to get home.*

Charlotte took a swig of water and Alex checked her watch again, in vain.

I don't know where this guy is?

Emmie leaned back in her seat, tilting the chair against the wall behind her so that the front legs lifted from the floor. But her eyes gave her away, nervously looking around while she fidgeted with the snap on the bib of her overalls.

Alex wasn't waiting on the good detective just to allow him to fumble this interview.

"Emmie, can you account for your whereabouts at the time Roy was murdered?"

"Can *you*?" Emmie snarled back at Alex.

"You didn't answer the question."

Emmie shifted forward in her seat, the chair legs smacking against the concrete. "I was here, like everyone else," she replied in a brazen tone.

"Can you be more specific? What exactly were you doing?"

Seymour Little returned with a cigar propped in his mouth and cobwebs in his hair.

Where has he been? He better not think he's going to light that up in here.

Emmie flashed the detective a nervous look. "I don't know," she said, replying to Alex's previous question.

"What do you mean you don't know?" Alex asked.

"I don't know, because I don't know exactly *when* Roy was killed."

She thinks she's smart.

Alex's eyes darted over to the detective as he finally sat down. *What are you going to do with that cigar, Seymour?* Then she flashed him a sidelong glance. *Geez, I'm starting to sound like Charlotte.*

Detective Little leaned forward, resting his elbows on the table, cigar wedged between his teeth. "Why don't you give us a rundown of your whole day, then."

Emmie's jaw twitched ever so slightly. "We all ate together, then later I walked over to the main house to greet our guests." She flicked her hand in Alex and Charlotte's direction. "Then I came back to the theater and was tasked with 'fetching' lunch." She sneered. "We all ate together. In here." She moved her face around in a circle, signifying the room they were in. "Like we do every day. I didn't see Roy at all after breakfast."

"Can anyone vouch for your whereabouts, during the day?" Detective Little studied Emmie's face. He tilted back in his chair, his eyes never leaving the suspect. "I need you to be honest with me. I have evidence that implicates you in Roy's murder."

Is he bluffing? Sure there's a bunch of little clues, but he didn't tell me if he had anything concrete.

"That's impossible," Emmie screeched, but her face paled. "Look, I swear, I didn't do it!"

She looked down at her hands and then back up to the detective. "We had a fight, but I didn't have anything to do with the murder. I swear!"

Detective Little started to speak, but Alex interrupted asking, "What did you fight about?"

"Breakfast. Like we do every day. It's not my fault that kid at the bistro always gets Roy's order wrong."

Changing tack, Alex asked, "Where were you when the weight almost killed Charlotte?" Alex asked. Emmie's eyes widened.

"You're not going to try to pin that on me too. I was waiting to go on stage, with the other actors. I was in my costume."

"You were the one who trashed the play on social media." The detective leaned closer, his voice low and dark.

How did he *know about that?*

"You can't prove that." Emmie scowled.

"Cheddar Chatter? Did you really think we wouldn't figure out it was you, money lady?" the detective shouted, and smacked his hand down on the table. Emmie jumped, and even Alex flinched at his antics.

He reached into his jacket pocket, pulled out an evidence bag and slammed a pair of dressmaker's shears—the murder weapon—down on the table, causing Emmie to recoil. "You killed Roy with these!"

Emmie flinched backward and threw her hands out. "Get those things away from me."

What is he doing? Those can't be the real scissors that came from Roy's neck? The sight of those scissors will stay with us for a long time!

"Why did you divulge the right-handed versus left-handed theory to the entire cast?" he asked with a steadfast gaze.

Emmie crossed her arms, her lips tightly closed.

"Well?" Alex demanded.

"I know my rights. I don't have to answer any of your questions. You're not the real police, and I'm not under arrest."

She sure is threading trouble.

"I may not be the real police, but he is." Alex jerked her thumb toward Detective Little.

At least I hope he is.

Little put the cigar down on the table, then picked up his half-empty coffee cup and slurped from it.

"And he's agreed to let me ask questions. And if you don't want to answer those questions, then you'll be arrested and taken to the police station to answer."

Emmie pulled a pair of scissors out of the pocket of her overalls. "I have mine right here. In fact, we *all* have a pair of them. A gift from Nona. So, how will you prove *those* were mine?" Emmie nodded to the detective's scissors and then set hers on the table. She flashed a smug look at Alex.

Oh boy! Checkmate. What are we going to do now?

13

LET'S GO EXPLORING

Exhausted and no closer to narrowing in on the true culprit, Alex settled into her sleeping room at the main house. She was just about to take Kibbles out of the crate and tuck her into bed with her when Charlotte, standing in the doorway, leaning against the jamb, said, "I really need food. The cheese and crackers only curbed my hunger."

"If you don't mind wandering around in our pajamas, we can grab something."

Charlotte looked down. "Clearly not," she said, gesturing to her own night clothes, a matching red-and-black checked flannel set.

Alex pulled a robe off the side chair and covered her nightshirt and shorts.

"Woof, woof."

"I'm going to go. Sorry, Kibbs, you need to stay in there a little longer."

Aiming for the kitchen as their destination, the two hustled down stairs and then walked the length of the hallway, peering into each of the offshoot rooms as they passed by. "This place is huge. I could definitely see myself living in a house like this,"

Charlotte said as they opened a door and discovered a billiard room.

"Not me. Even number 1 is too big for me," Alex replied.

"Thank you for letting me shine tonight. It felt good to be the star of the show."

"Of course, I've never meant for—"

"I know. It wasn't you, it was me. I felt overshadowed, but *I* chose my path in life, and I don't regret going the hard way." Charlotte winked.

The two women pushed through a swinging door into the kitchen.

"Wow, it's surprisingly modern. For some reason I expected the kitchen to be vintage." Charlotte ran her hand across the granite countertop and opened the fridge. With the door open, she peeked around inside, and looking toward Alex, asked, "Do you want to explore the Bat Cave some more?"

Alex smiled. "That's a very mischievous look you have there, Charlotte."

"It's not like we'd be intruding. It all belongs to you now."

Charlotte carefully balanced a bunch of dishes and closed the fridge with a bump from her backside.

"What is all that?"

"Your guess is as good as mine. I'm thinking there must be something here we'll find agreeable."

Alex took the top two bowls, which were wrapped in reusable cloth covers, and set them on the counter while Charlotte laid out two more plates wrapped the same way.

Alex removed the floral covers, revealing a bowl of macaroni and cheese and a bowl of cranberry chicken salad. "Dibs on the chicken salad."

"Do you eat anything but?"

"Yes, I eat pizza," Alex joked.

"Fine by me, I have dibs on this plate." She held out the dish for Alex to inspect.

"Looks like a precursor to an Easter feast."

Charlotte grinned. "Yum!" She stepped over to the microwave and set the timer. "Did you see any more online? Any critiques for the play, I mean?"

"I haven't had a minute to check my messages, never mind my social media. Do you think it will get much attention?" Alex spun around, searching. There—a bread box was right behind her with a plate of fresh-baked bread inside.

"I would think the actors would post something. If nothing else, maybe we'll find a clue for the investigation." Charlotte doubled back to the fridge and pulled out two old-fashioned glass bottles of root beer.

"For sure." After opening a few drawers, Alex found the silverware.

The microwave beeped, and Charlotte handled her plate like a hot potato while Alex set a fork and knife down for Charlotte and then made herself a half sandwich.

"Mmm, so delicious." Alex mumbled as she dove into her sandwich.

"Napkins?" Charlotte asked, with a mouthful of steaming mashed potatoes.

Alex grabbed the end of the paper towel roll and tugged. She handed one to Charlotte and then wiped her own mouth. "I didn't realize how hungry *I* was."

"Let's finish up so we can go explore." Charlotte spooned a scoop of green bean casserole into her mouth.

"Do you know if there is another way down to the *lair*?" Alex asked. She finished her last bite and cleared the crumbs from the counter.

Charlotte rinsed her plate and put it in the dishwasher. "Not that I saw, but we can look for a stairwell."

"Don't you feel like we'll be snooping around in someone else's business?"

"Heck no! This secret society business is fun."

"I'll leave it to you, then."

"Come on, there's no harm." Charlotte dragged Alex out of the kitchen by the hand, and skimmed her other hand against the wall, feeling as she walked.

"What are you doing?"

"I'm looking for another secret passageway."

The wall clicked, and a small door popped open revealing a very sophisticated control panel.

"Aha, I think there's an elevator here." Charlotte pushed a red down arrow button, and the whole wall panel slid to the right, revealing an elevator cage behind it. "This place is so cool!" Charlotte squealed with glee.

"I hope it's going to take us to the right place."

Charlotte wrinkled her brow. "Where else would it take us?" she said as she pushed the cage door aside. "Get in."

Alex stepped into the vintage elevator, and Charlotte clanked the cage door closed behind them. She pressed the corresponding down arrow button, and the lift descended before coming to a stop with a rumbling thud.

Alex heaved the antique door open and stepped out into the cavernous chamber. The room was dimly lit, and she spied things she hadn't noticed the first time she was down there. Rows of shelves lined with old books and antique gadgets. And then a small telescope that was perched in the corner pointed to an antique roll top desk covered with old maps and journals.

Alex picked up an old leather-bound book and flipped through the pages. The handwriting was illegible and the ink was faint. Her gaze danced around the scrolled handwriting. *Nona's.* Though the words appeared familiar, the coded sentences were unknown to her. *What does it say?* She ran her finger over the embossed Society of Six symbol. *What did I miss that would have prevented your murder, Nona?*

The journal was, in a way, a treasure map to a secret world. *Of what? Espionage and adventure?*

She needed to get out of this room and start piecing together the clues of Roy's death before their time in Mishap was up. *Sure, I saved Charlotte once, but I failed to save Nona. Not a stellar record.*

"Careful, Alex, that's a dart gun, complete with poisoned darts."

Alex had been lost in her thoughts and unknowingly leaned dangerously close to the weapon. "How do you know that?" Alex asked.

Charlotte tapped on the plaque attached to the pedestal. "It says so, right here."

"Oh." Alex backed up.

"Did you see the embroidered handkerchief?" Charlotte asked, tilting her head and nodding toward a display case to her right. "It was owned by one of the original six members."

Alex stepped around Charlotte and peered into the glass display case and then around the area. "I think I see a sample of Nona's work over there." Alex pointed across the spacious room. Charlotte walked over to the display.

Alex shivered and tightened the belt on her robe. "Let's head up, I think I've had enough for one day."

Alex lay in bed, her body tense and her mind racing, failing to shake off the remnants of a bad dream she woken abruptly from. She wiped sweat from her brow with her shirt sleeve. Kibbles snored peacefully on the pillow beside her. This nightmare was more vivid and lifelike, unlike her last one where Nona had appeared and given her a message.

In this dream, she'd been crossing the stage, running from the killer. She had sensed her time was running out and was terrified.

Lying in the king-sized bed, she tried to steady her racing heart by breathing in slow, controlled breaths. Her mind wandered back to the other strange elements of her dream. Marilyn Monroe had flashed across the stage in Alex's mind, Marilyn's iconic blonde hair and red lips stood out starkly against the dark background of the dream. Uncle Sam had been there too. His pointed finger wagged in admonition as he scolded Alex for something she couldn't quite recall. And of course Kibbles and Chirp had made a cameo. Both of them darted around her feet as she ran, their meows and barks blended into a confusing cacophony.

Alex sat up and shook her head. The real-life play was bizarre enough, but she couldn't make any sense of the dream or what her imagination had been trying to tell her. She took a deep breath and lay back down, covering her head with her pillow, a vision of a mysterious shadowy figure, the killer, chasing her still fresh in her mind. There was something wrong with the way they ran while chasing her.

The stage led outside. It's like they were chasing me out of the house. What does that mean?

She was too exhausted to puzzle it out. Instead, she texted Hawk.

ALEX:

Play went off without a hitch.

Well, one tiny hitch.

Missing you.

Her only hope now was that the rest of her sleep would be peaceful and uneventful. But even as she drifted off, she couldn't shake the notion that something was lurking, just around the corner, waiting to pounce.

14

NEW YEAR'S EVE

The first thing Alex did when she woke was grab her phone. Rolling onto her side, she pulled the charger cord out of the bottom of the phone and checked for a reply from Hawk. Two texts from separate senders. She pulled up Hawk's first.

HAWK:

Missing you also.

Are you having fun?

He misses me! Alex held the phone to her heart. Warmth rushed up her cheeks as they flushed, and she read the message again.

She quickly typed out a response, her fingers tapping away on the screen. As she hit send, Alex was flooded with excitement and now ready for the rest of the day.

ALEX:

Nothing like a murder mystery!

Then she pulled up the second text. To her surprise it was from an unknown number.

UNKNOWN:

It's not who you think.

It's not who? Emmie, Comare, Liam, Nona? Is this about the case in Mishap, or the cases back home?

The phone chirped, and another text from Hawk came in distracting her from her barrage of thoughts.

HAWK:

Have you heard from Doc?

Hawk was always on a case. This day, it was their case back in Salem.

ALEX:

About the fingerprints? No, nothing yet.

I just received another unknown number text.

ALEX:

I'll forward it to you.

I've too much on my mind to deal with it right now.

HAWK:

Okay. I'll let you know if I hear anything.

Or find anything.

ALEX:

It's probably better you don't. I have my hands full here.

HAWK:

Are you ok?

ALEX:

I'm fine.

HAWK:

FINE is a four letter word.

ALEX:

Ha! Nothing I can't handle.

HAWK:

Good. Let's talk later.

I'm getting on a plane to head home.

Be safe.

ALEX:

You too!

Alex pulled up the mystery text again, frowning. She rolled out of bed and peeked out the window. She had no clue where this text was coming from, or the others she had received while on the cruise and also back home, and even worse, how the sender knew her every move.

Kibbles stirred. "Woof, woof."

Does the dog know what I'm thinking too?

"But you have to get out of bed, you little mutt! Come on. Let's go for a walk. Where'd I put your sweater?"

Kibbles jumped down and ran under the bed. She dragged out her sweater, let go of it and barked once.

"Why thank you. How'd that get under there?"

"Meeeow!" Chirp caterwauled from under the bed.

Alex bent down. "How'd *you* get under there?"

She opened the door, and Chirp slinked out from under the bed, his tail curling around Alex's leg, then the bed frame, and finally the doorjamb before he ran out.

Dressed in her favorite leggings and her Boston sweatshirt, she instantly relaxed a fraction but looked over her shoulder anyway before leaving the room.

. . .

Outside, in the courtyard, the sun was shining. Although a peaceful morning to most, Alex's mind was churning. *Someone has murdered one person already, and tried for Charlotte, or me. Who? And why? And why isn't it who I think?* She was also still disturbed by her dream. *Why wasn't Charlotte in it?*

In the light of day, she realized there had been a ruckus in the background that she hadn't been aware of when she'd woken in the middle of the night. *What was it?*

While Kibbles did her business, Alex chewed on her lip, trying to hear the strange noises from her dream. Nearby, Chirp circled a large oak tree in the courtyard.

Laughter. It was laughter. Mocking me.

Like in a movie when the person gets up on stage and realizes they have no pants on. She squinted her eyes, trying to remember. *How's that going to help you* hear *a voice of laughter?*

Kibbles came to her side, and they walked to the left around the block that encompassed the house.

Laughter, but who . . .

"Let's go get Charlotte, Kibbles, and see if she's come to any better conclusions."

The text said it isn't who I think it is. But how do they know who it is or who I *think it is?*

Alex walked through the front door, the cold winter air trailing behind her as she cradled her furry companion. The smell of bacon and freshly brewed coffee wafted through the air, making both their stomachs growl in anticipation.

She started to make her way to the kitchen, but the usually demure hallway was filled with streamers. Liam stood atop a ladder as he hung a large banner that read 'Happy New Year!' in bold, sparkling letters. Alex raised an eyebrow in confusion. *Why is he decorating like this?*

"Good morning, Alex!"

"Good morning, Liam." Alex set the dog on the floor. "Please tell me you aren't hosting a party?"

"Why yes, we are. I'm decorating for the New Year's Eve party tonight." Liam gestured to the decorations around him. "I wanted everything to be perfect for our guests."

Alex groaned. "We need to find Roy's killer before we have a house full of guests. Don't you think?"

Kibbles barked in alarm, and Liam replied, "I have faith in you." With a smile, he climbed down from the ladder.

Alex shook her head, scooped up her pup, and walked toward the dining room, where she overheard Charlotte and Detective Little arguing.

Inside the dining room, the detective greeted her, "Alex."

Alex sat next to Charlotte at the table and put Kibbles in the empty chair on the other side of herself.

"Morning, Detective. Is everything okay?" The tension in the air was thick. She eyed Charlotte with a 'behave yourself' glare.

Charlotte pursed her lips and turned her head away.

Alex sniffed the air appreciatively. The sweet aroma of cinnamon and sugar brought a smile to her face as she surveyed the spread of food: pancakes, French toast, and waffles, all piled high on fine china serving plates. "Hmm, none of that for you, Kibbles. I guess some scrambled eggs won't hurt." Alex scooped some from a large platter, preparing two plates, one for her and one for Kibbles. She poured herself a glass of thick peach smoothie, the glass frosting up as she poured.

Charlotte snuck Kibbles a piece of bacon.

"I saw that."

Charlotte feigned innocence.

"Not too much bacon. It's not good for her! Do you want to deal with more of her gas?" Alex asked, turning to catch Charlotte feeding Kibbles a small piece of sausage.

"What?" Charlotte shrugged. "She has to eat!"

"I'll put her in your room later, and you'll think twice next time before you feed her like that." She smiled fondly at both the dog and her friend.

Charlotte stuck out her tongue and tossed Kibbles another sausage scrap.

"So, what did I miss?" Alex asked, to no one in particular, changing the subject.

"Did you see the headline? 'Enchanting Actress Captivates Mishap.' Can you believe someone described me as enchanting?"

Alex smiled, "Of course." She replied, before tucking into her plate of eggs and then piled on some bacon and sausage.

"How about the party?" Charlotte asked Alex, who was mid-sip of her puréed fruit drink that had dribbled down her chin.

Alex wiped her face and said, "I saw." She hung her head in defeat. "That means we need to solve this murder before the party tonight, or someone else could be in danger."

The detective fidgeted, listening to their conversation.

Charlotte looked at him and then at her phone again and giggled.

Alex rolled her eyes. *Why is no one taking this seriously?*

Charlotte picked at her food until her phone chimed again, and a wide smile broke across her face.

Who is she texting with?

Alex's own phone buzzed. She glanced down at the screen,

which displayed another text from Hawk. Her heart skipped a beat as she eagerly opened the message.

HAWK:

Are you going to be delayed?

ALEX:

Not if I can help it.

I have to solve this murder before a New Year's Eve Party tonight.

I hate being away.

From you, is what she wanted to type. Butterflies fluttered around in her stomach. She'd fallen hard for Hawk on their last date. She was tired of not talking to him while he was on a case, never mind being away from him for any length of time. The next message was short and sweet, making her smile from ear to ear.

HAWK:

We'll ring in the new year when you get back.

ALEX:

Yes, please!

HAWK:

How's our pooch?

Giddiness overcame Alex, and she gazed down at Kibbles. *Our pooch*.

ALEX:

A stinker, but good.

HAWK:

Great. Do you want me to run any names of the guests?

ALEX:

I don't even know who's coming, but I'm on alert.

HAWK:

I trust you can handle yourself. Be safe!

Charlotte giggled again, fixated on her phone.

"You two are acting like lovesick teenagers. Are you ready to get on with this investigation or what?" the detective asked.

"Woof, woof."

Alex set her phone aside. "You go, we'll be out in a minute."

Little placed his napkin down on the table beside his plate and pushed his chair away back. He stood and walked out without another word.

"We can't leave this to the *good* detective," Charlotte whispered.

"I know. Look, I wanted to tell you, I received one of those mysterious text messages last night."

Charlotte put her fork down and stared intently at Alex.

"It said 'It's not who you think,' but for some reason, I don't think this text has anything to do with Roy's murder or killer. I mean, how could it?"

"I don't know. It's pretty creepy, though, like someone's watching your every move."

"I know, I checked out the window, half expecting to see an ominous black car outside, like in the movies. Then I checked over my shoulder before I left the room. Paranoid much?"

"I can understand how you would be a bit paranoid. It was a crazy year, and you're not going to be settled until you have all the answers."

"Regardless, I want to be out of here and on the road Monday morning."

Charlotte popped the last of her breakfast into her mouth.

"Then we need to wrap this up!" she said, chewing. "According to Emmie, everyone had the same scissors gifted to them by Nona. We could check and see who's missing a pair?"

Kibbles barked twice in disagreement.

Alex scratched the dog's chin. "We could, but I suspect that based on Emmie's actions regarding the left- versus right-hand questioning, she's already made sure everyone has a pair. And even if not, we wouldn't really be able to tell whose are whose," Alex replied.

"She's meddlesome. And sketchy. Why would she want to block us from solving this unless she's guilty?" Charlotte got up from the table, grabbed her plate and cleaned spilled coffee off the tablecloth. "Isn't it always the one who inserts themselves into the case who's guilty?"

"On TV it usually is." Alex laughed, clearing her place setting and checking to see that Kibbles had eaten her food. "One of the actors mentioned a sleuthing group, Emmie's likely part of it."

"Amateurs!" Charlotte exclaimed mockingly, and put her plate on the dirty dish trolley.

"Funny." Alex smiled and did the same. Kibbles jumped down off her chair. "We're missing something. There doesn't seem to be any connection between Roy and someone trying to hurt you . . . or me. Apparently, everyone had motive to kill Roy, but no one had a motive to kill you, so that's inconclusive." Alex could hear Charlotte mocking the detective's words though she didn't make a peep, for once. "And despite our efforts, we can't piece together a solid motive for this crime."

"How about the strange text message you received?" Charlotte asked as they walked out of the dining room, Kibbles at their heels.

Alex flipped the light off behind them. "I don't know who it is, but it *does* seem like they have my back."

Walking down the hall to the front door, Charlotte said, "Things sure are exciting when you're around, Alex."

"That's an understatement."

"I'm gonna go up." Charlotte pointed to the stairway. "I can't take any more of that detective today."

Kibbles darted around, her tail wagging happily as she sniffed around the floor.

Alex picked up the dog and handed her to Charlotte. "Would you take her out to do her business and then put her in the crate? And I'll deal with the detective."

"Deal!" Charlotte started toward the front door with Kibbles, stopped and turned. "I don't see how Hawk hasn't been able to find anything on the sender, if it's the same one as before. What kind of PI is he?" Charlotte asked and smiled. Alex knew Charlotte was just being her usual feisty self.

"I suspect, much like this secret society business, if, *and when* someone wants us to know, we'll know."

"Or we'll stumble upon it, eventually," Charlotte added.

No, not stumble upon it. I'm going to figure it out. If it kills me!

15

A SPY AMONGST US

ALEX MET THE DETECTIVE ON THE PORCH, AND TOGETHER they walked through the courtyard. The sun was finally shining bright, and the slight breeze was crisp, but negligible.

It was time to stop playing the detective's game. She faced him. "All right, I'm leaving soon. Do you want to tell me why you have been pretending to be *Detective Seymour Little* all this time?"

"I appreciate that you didn't give away my secret. I wasn't sure you'd roll with it, when I handed you my real business card," Detective Bronco said. He held out his hand. "Aames Bronco, and it's nice to truly meet you, Alexandra Bailey."

She shook his hand. "I'm ready for this drama to be over." She said and continued walking.

As they rounded the big oak tree, a faint whizzing zipped past Alex's ear. Her heart raced, and she looked toward Bronco with wide eyes. He had pinched a dart between his fingers, his hand beside her head. He held it up, to examine it, and scowled.

"What the—How did you catch that?" Alex stared at him in bewilderment.

Who is this guy?

"Poisoned," he said, and his eyes scanned the courtyard searching for a culprit.

Alex gaped, still in shock, unbelieving that she had almost been hit with a poisoned dart while walking to the theater.

"How do you know it's poisoned?"

"See this tip? See how it's a slightly darker shade than the rest? That means it's been saturated with a liquid poison. It's very effective." He grimaced. "Someone has it out for you, Alex. And now, I'm even more sure that sandbag was meant for *you*." He grabbed Alex's arm. "Quick, let's get inside."

Detective Bronco pulled her into an alcove and scanned their surroundings again. His hand slid from her arm to her hand, and he pulled her toward the back door of the theater. Together they beelined it inside.

Backstage, the detective turned to her, his expression softening with concern. "Are you okay?"

Alex nodded mutely. She gazed at the detective, her eyes searching his, bewildered but grateful.

"That came from—" She stopped herself before revealing where the dart may have come from. Likely Liam's lair. She and Charlotte had seen the dart gun and poisoned darts amongst the Society of Six artifacts.

The harrowing moment was dispelled by the cat and dog rolling around on the floor, and playfully nipping at each other. "How'd you get out of your crate, you little rascal?"

There is no way she could have gotten out on her own.

"Did you teach the dog how to get out of her crate?" Alex asked the cat, half-jokingly.

The cat blinked at her, as if to say, 'What do you think?' and then chirped one long melodic chirp.

"I knew it!" Alex shook her head in disbelief. "I can't believe it, you're such a naughty boy."

Kibbles barked her three-alarm call at the cat, and the cat sat looking back at Alex with a defiant gleam in his eyes.

But despite her scolding, Alex couldn't help but smile at the sight of the two animals together. They were an odd pair, but they were playing surprisingly well. And in a way, she was intrigued that the cat taught the dog a new trick. It was a reminder of how smart and resourceful this pair was.

What else will they do?

"Wait, how did the animals get into the theater?" Alex questioned aloud.

"I can answer that," Emmie said from behind Alex. "The vomitory exit."

Alex turned, and Emmie pointed to the inconspicuous opening.

"That's enough. Stop right there," Detective Bronco raised his voice to Emmie. "You're going to have to come with me, miss." He walked over to Emmie, holding up a pair of handcuffs, and flashed his wallet and badge. "You're under arrest for the murder of Roy Ziegler."

She stared at his identification. "Bronco? I thought your name was Little?" Emmie's brows drew together in confusion. He cuffed the woman. "I was just being helpful. You can't arrest me!" Emmie cried out. "You've got nothing on me," she snarled, like a cornered tiger, spit flying from her mouth.

Wow, this is abrupt? Is this part of the act or real life?

"I pinpointed Roy's death to just before Alex and Charlotte arrived in Mishap," the detective reported.

"But she was in the house when we arrived," Alex mentioned to the detective.

"Precisely—this vomitory is connected to the house via a secret tunnel. That very few people including her know about."

"I love this place!" Charlotte popped up next to Alex with a bag of chips in her hand.

Emmie frowned. "This doesn't even make sense. I could've just as easily walked over, through the courtyard, and let myself in. I have a key."

"I'm afraid that doesn't help your case at all," the detective responded, taking her out in cuffs.

Charlotte crunched on a potato chip and brushed crumbs off her shirt. She sat in a nearby theater seat. "Now who's going to bring us coffee?"

Alex shook her head at her friend's sarcastic question and suppressed a smile.

Bronco walked Emmie out through the front entrance.

Charlotte grinned a big cheese-eating grin and leaned back toward Alex. "Do you at least want to see where the secret passageway comes out?"

"Fine, we'll take Kibbles back as well. Kibbles!"

Kibbles ran up to Alex.

"She can show the way, she knows now too." Charlotte chuckled.

"Let's go, then, show me."

The trio exited the theater through the vomitory tunnel which was pitch black with no adornments on the walls. They approached a door at the end with a dimly lit exit sign. Standing next to Alex, Charlotte held her hand up to stop Alex from going through the door. "That one is an actual exit, that leads out to the opposite side of the building from the courtyard. That's not where we want to go. But you'll have to check it out later, there's a massive quilt mural painted on the facade. It's grand."

"How—Never mind. Nona's doing, I assume."

Charlotte waggled her eyebrows. "Yup, *and* she's part of the mural too. Hand-stitching a Grandmother's Flower Garden quilt. I don't want to spoil it. You have to see it for yourself."

"I guess I shouldn't be surprised. Nona was always over-the-top." Alex smiled. "Where are we supposed to go, then?" Alex looked around. "I can't see anything." There were no other doors at the end of the hallway where they stood.

Kibbles nosed the felt covered wall, and a hidden door, no bigger than the pets, sprang open.

"It's neat, there's a spot at pet height to get the little pet door to open, and another at human height." Charlotte beamed, seriously entertained by all the mystery and intrigue of the property.

"How did she know where the secret pet door was?" Alex asked Charlotte.

"I think she sensed it, or Chirp really did show her how to do it." Charlotte shrugged. "Reach out, right in front of you."

Alex put her hand out straight, vertically to where Kibbles had touched the wall, and it clicked. "I just pressed it and it popped open." Alex marveled.

"Cool, huh? Follow Kibbles," Charlotte said, and nudged Alex forward.

"Chirp. Chirp," the cat slinked by and ran ahead of Kibbles, Alex and Charlotte.

"Woof, woof." she barked and then followed him into the underground passageway.

Alex opened the full-size door wider and asked, "Where does it lead, Charlotte?"

"I'm not going to tell you, that would ruin the surprise."

They walked through the tunnel, not having to duck at all. Alex felt her hand along the massive stone block walls. A string of construction lights overhead lit the way as Alex focused her eyes in the dark. A slight chill and a staleness in the air made the tunnel all the more cloak-and-dagger-ish. Alex walked into a cobweb and spat, "Puh!" and blew out, "Blah!" She stopped to wipe her face. Charlotte encouraged her forward and they quickly came to the base of a set of stone steps.

Kibbles bounded up the stairs, Alex and Charlotte trailing behind. At the top, the dog reached up and pawed the wall. Another small pet door opened, revealing the light of a room, and Kibbles passed through. Alex put up her hands, feeling the blank, soft wall until something clicked. This wall rolled back into the wall and disappeared, and they entered the billiard room. The very same one they had poked their heads into during their late-night exploration.

Inside the room, Charlotte tapped something on the wall and the door slid back into place. The door was seamless and looked like one of the panels on the wall, if they hadn't known about it, they would never have found it.

"Did the cat show you this secret?" Alex asked the small pooch, who was staring up at her intently.

The cat chirped, walking along the top of the pool table, and then caterwauled.

"I guess that says it all."

Liam brought drinks to Alex, who was sitting in her favorite oversized comfy chaise, and Charlotte, who was pacing the room. Kibbles lounged in Chirp's bed by the ornate fireplace screen.

Liam sat on the sofa and crossed his legs. He sipped appreciatively from a glass of scotch. "Well done, ladies!"

"We didn't really do much?" Charlotte guffawed.

"Well, the murderer has been apprehended, and now we get

back to Society business—which is partially why I invited you to Mishap."

Alex sniffed at her brandy before taking a swig. "I'm still puzzled by how Kibbles could've been trained."

Liam swirled his glass. "I spoke to Nona just before she was . . ."

"Sorry, I don't mean to interrupt you, but how? How did you communicate with her? I combed through the phone records after Nona's murder, looking for strange numbers and found no record of this or any Georgia numbers."

"I have a Massachusetts cellular number for precisely that reason," Liam replied.

"Like a burner phone?" Charlotte asked, making faces in a gilded oval mirror.

"Ignore her! Sorry, continue please," Alex insisted.

Suppressing a grin, Liam turned his attention back to Alex and continued, "I spoke to Nona, and she suspected Lilith was planted by the Comare in a misguided attempt to infiltrate the neighborhood and the Society. So the only way Kibbles could be trained, if not by Lilith, was by the Comare."

"Or Rebecca?" Alex whispered. *She is the last known Society member unaccounted for.*

"Kibbles is a spy?" Charlotte squealed, and then crossed her eyes in the mirror.

"Woof, woof!" Kibbles lifted her head in protest.

"Kibbles isn't a spy. That's ridiculous."

"Woof," the pup replied in gratitude.

"What are you doing over there?" Alex asked Charlotte.

Charlotte turned around. "I don't know. Making faces for the camera behind the mirror."

"I think this place is warping your reality."

Liam chuckled. "There's no one behind that mirror, no camera. I'm sorry to tell you, it's just a plain old mirror."

"Boo-hoo." Charlotte pouted and plonked down on the sofa.

"Okay, but how could the Comare train Kibbles? How would she get access to the Society's training, assuming it's a trade secret?"

"It is. Well, it's *supposed* to be secret. It's taken me a while to determine the answer to that," Liam replied. "Now, this is just my speculation, of course. It will need to be proven, if and when we find her, but I believe this all started with Rebecca Briggs in New York." Liam uncrossed his legs and set his lowball glass down.

Charlotte finished her chardonnay and refilled her wineglass before Liam continued.

"My theory is, the Comare found out about the Society, either on her own or from Rebecca while she was living in New York."

"That would explain the New York connection," Alex murmured.

"If Rebecca, or Winnefred Winters, whoever she is, was one of the original members of the Society, why would she share trade secrets with the Mafia?" Charlotte asked.

Alex's stomach flipped, and she paled. Her hands clammy she gaped at Charlotte.

"Come on, Alex, it's no secret that Alex Bailey was a Mafia lawyer." Charlotte chuckled.

Alex tossed a throw pillow at her. "I was not!"

"Maybe you didn't know for sure, but you suspected it. Isn't that why you left?" Charlotte was beginning to display the effects of her alcohol consumption, and the last time the two were inebriated, she and Charlotte had fought.

Liam stiffened. "Yes, it's no coincidence you were hired by the law firm of Weitz & Romano, Alex."

"But why, and how would Nona have allowed that?" Alex

asked. She wrapped herself in both quilts from the back of the chair.

"Why—better to keep you close, since you were destined to become the new head of the Society. How—Nona didn't know, until recently."

Alex guzzled her brandy, and Liam continued.

"I believe two things: One—it's entirely possible that your old boss Remo's sister Eleanor—the Comare's daughter was killed on Spruce Street by Nona, your parents and Rebecca. Now, Nona never confirmed this to me, for good reason, and there's nothing in the Society records about it, but it is the only thing that makes sense to me."

"What's the second thing?" Charlotte asked, crossing her legs on the sofa cushion.

"Your parents' death was not an accident, Alex."

Alex squeezed the bolster pillow on her chair. "I've always wondered." Tears welled up in her eyes and as much as she wanted to stop them, she couldn't. She heaved a sigh of relief and let them flow. "If you'll excuse me, Liam, I'm going to go upstairs and freshen up."

16

NEW YEAR'S EVE

LATER THAT EVENING, AFTER A GOOD CRY ON HER PILLOW and more questions, ones she hadn't been prepared to ask herself, Alex descended the grand staircase—composed, for now. Twinkling lights flickered, and joyous laughter emanated from the lower floor. She smoothed her dress nervously before making her way to the first-floor landing. For the second time in as many days, she was dressed in an evening gown, courtesy of the costume department—this one, a red strapless dress covered in sequins.

Liam greeted her warmly. "Alex." He took her arm, smiling at her appreciatively. He handed her a glass of champagne—the hallway was lined with tables covered in a lavish buffet of gourmet treats.

Alex glanced around the foyer decorated with metallic accents and shimmering lights that evoked a sense of glamor. The grand entrance to the ballroom featured an archway adorned with black and gold balloons.

Liam leaned in. "I have to say, you look just like your mom."

She smiled. "I haven't been told that in a long time. Thank you, Liam."

"Your dad was a good man," he said, his voice softening. "We only worked together for a short time, but he talked about you and your mom all the time."

Alex's smile faded. "Hard to believe it's been over twenty years. I miss them so much, and Nona too." She reached to catch a tear forming in the corner of her eye.

"I know," Liam replied, patting her hand. "But your parents would be proud of the person you've become. You've accomplished so much. You've made a real difference in this world."

Alex peered up at the disco ball hanging from the center of the ceiling. Flickering candles and a glittering vase of flowers stood on the chunky mantel of the fireplace. Her heart softened. "Thank you, that means a lot."

"Know that I'm here for you, now."

The house was buzzing with activity; her ears were infused with laughter and music.

A room packed with potential benefactors. Liam should be fleecing them all for donations.

Alex sipped from her glass of champagne and glanced around at the crowd. To her amazement, Liam's New Year's Eve party was in full swing, but loneliness lingered beneath her cool exterior despite the activities of the past few days and her determination to enjoy herself. She'd traveled a thousand miles, through ten states, just to find the answers that might explain why her life had been so derailed this past year. And all she could think about was how much she missed Hawk.

What is he doing at this exact moment? Is he thinking of me too?

Liam wandered off and as the night wore on, Alex found herself swept around from guest to guest, and in conversation with Liam's acquaintances, many of whom had also attended the play. They chatted about New Year's resolutions and reminisced about the year that had passed—all the while Alex was a million miles away, puzzling out the events of the past week and the past year.

She spied the squat detective lurking by the piano. *Please, no show tunes!*

Alex peered around looking for Charlotte, who was no where in sight.

As she scanned the crowded room, she couldn't shake the suspicion that something wasn't right about Emmie being the killer. She'd been pondering the interviews all day, and had the notion that they'd arrested the wrong person. Emmie didn't have any motive different than any other cast member.

Come to think of it, I don't really know what the motive to kill Roy is at all.

Sure, Emmie is probably not a very nice person, or at least she's very disgruntled. She just stood by while Wallace fainted. She didn't do much when the detective was fake choking. Harrison, the lighting and sound guy, was the one who saved him. He didn't really, though, he just acted like he was going to, and he isn't even one of the actors, is he? Emmie wanted to question Harrison herself, but I stopped her. Could it be Harrison?

As Alex pondered, the lights overhead dimmed and the volume of the music increased.

What would his motive be? Wait, the lights, could it be? Her eyes widened. *Yes, it's got to be him.*

Alex weaved through the crowd to Detective Bronco. She narrowed her eyes. "We've got the wrong person in custody."

"I know," he replied. "And the real killer is here."

"Harrison," the spoke simultaneously, an eerie whisper that passed between them.

"He claimed he was at the control board at the time of the murder, but we never established exactly what time Roy was killed," Bronco said.

Upset that she'd been wrong, Alex added, "I dismissed

Harrison, because he turned up the lights. I assumed he was at the control board, like he said. But no, when Charlotte and I first met him he had some sort of remote control, so he could have been anywhere in the theater."

The detective nodded sagely.

"But why did he do it?" Alex muttered, not expecting an answer as she scanned the crowded New Year's Eve party, searching for Harrison.

"Jealousy!" the detective replied.

Suddenly, from across the room, the familiar face of an older woman caught her eye, momentarily distracting her. It was someone she recognized but couldn't place from where. The woman glared back at her, and a jolt of unease hit Alex.

There's no time for this, I need to catch the real *killer.*

She spotted the Harrison, the lighting and sound guy, at the pop-up bar in the far corner of the grand room. As she pushed her way through the throngs of partygoers, her heart raced with adrenaline.

Alex approached Harrison. "I have a quick question for you," she said, her voice casual.

"Hey, Alex, sure, what can I do for you?" Harrison replied, and took a sip of a foamy beer.

Detective Bronco came up behind her, and Harrison's smile faltered.

Alex asked, "Are you able to control the theater lights remotely?"

Harrison's face paled, and he dropped his beer, splashing it all over Alex's feet. Several people nearby jumped back in surprise, some at the sound of glass hitting the floor and a few, as the cold, frothy beverage hit their ankles.

Detective Bronco grabbed Harrison's arm before he could run. "You're under arrest for the murder of Roy Ziegler." Harrison resisted, but the detective slapped the handcuffs on him, ignoring the surprised gasps from guests nearby. He ushered Harrison through the crowd and out of the party.

"You coming?" the detective asked Alex.

"No, there's something here I need to deal with." Alex scanned the room for the woman she had spotted earlier. *Where have I seen her before?*

She stepped into the hallway and Liam passed by. Alex reached out for his arm. "Liam, do you know the blonde woman in the black dress?"

He looked around. "There are quite a few women, blondes in black dresses. Can you be more specific?"

"She was elderly, had a brooch by her shoulder, I didn't get a good look at it. But she glared at me sharply, and I can't help but think I've seen her somewhere before."

He pursed his lips. "Hmm, maybe she was a guest for the play? Many of the people here tonight were at the unveiling ceremony and the debut."

"Maybe," Alex murmured. As she stood there lost in thought, a bustle at the front door caught her attention.

Liam looked up in the direction of the commotion. "The Comare!"

"She's here?" Alex questioned, and they both hurried through the crowd. "Stop that woman," Alex yelled. But it was too late; the woman vanished out the door.

The woman was long gone by the time Alex and Liam made it to the door. They both stood on the front porch, scanning the street and the courtyard.

"Where'd she go?" Alex asked.

"I don't see her."

Alex shivered in her strapless gown.

"Let's get you back inside. It's probably not safe out here."

Once inside, Alex hovered by the fire in the library. "How? Why, Liam?"

"She must be behind the attacks on you. She's a long way from home." He flashed a concerned glance. "During the play, you were the target. And the poisoned dart."

"How did you know about the dart? I never said anything."

"I'm in cahoots with the detective. Don't let this butler's routine fool you, I know and see everything. Well, almost everything." A pained expression crossed his face.

"What does that mean?" Alex asked.

"I have the whole place under surveillance. Well, I thought I did, until Roy was killed."

"The cameras didn't catch it?" Alex asked.

"Sadly, no. I've been reviewing the footage all week. There were a few blind spots. The detective and I fixed the problem, but unfortunately, it was too late for Roy. Using our surveillance weakness to his advantage, Harrison was able to kill Roy without anyone noticing. He's pretty savvy when it comes to lighting and sound . . . and video!"

The crowd erupted in a countdown: ten, nine, eight, seven . . .

Alex and Liam, joined his guests as the clock struck midnight. An overhead projector broadcasted a ball dropping, from somewhere around the world, onto a huge screen. The ballroom erupted in chaos; partygoers cheered and clinked their glasses, couples kissed, and Alex gave Liam a polite smile.

Her phone buzzed next to her heart.

HAWK:

Happy New Year. Be safe.

17

THE BIRDS

ALEX WOKE TO HAPPY LITTLE SONGBIRDS CHATTERING outside her window. She rolled out of bed and peeked out the curtains, holding them open just enough to spy several tiny kinglets. The birds were frantically twitching around on the branches of the tree that was growing close to the side of the house.

I could use some of that energy this morning.

As if one of the tiny balls of gray feathers heard her thoughts, it popped onto the windowsill just long enough to flick its wings a couple of times for her before flying off back to its friends.

Alex yawned, released the curtain and stretched her arms over her head. "Come on, sleepyhead!" She flung the covers away, revealing the small bundle of fur that was Kibbles.

With one eye open, Kibbles let out a half-hearted woof and covered her eye with her paw.

"Come on. Let's go out to potty."

Alex threw a hoodie on and slipped into her jeans. Not bothering to untie them or even put socks on first, she struggle to wedge her feet into her shoes. She grabbed the bedpost, trying to push her heels in and Kibbles finally sat up. "Let's go."

Kibbles jumped off the bed and followed her down to the first floor and out the front door.

Happily watching the dog nose around the courtyard for the perfect spot to do her business, Alex bent to smell the spicy fragrance of the Sweetshrub. She couldn't have anticipated what happened next. Footsteps approached from behind. As she stood, a pair of strong arms wrapped around her neck, choking her. Her heart raced. She tried to scream, but no sound came out. Panic set in as Alex struggled to break free, but her attacker's grip only tightened.

Kibbles whined and went nuts about her owner's distress, continuing her alarm call repeatedly. Instinctively, Alex reached back and grabbed her attacker's hair, pulling with all her strength. A sharp pain pulled at her arm muscle as she ripped out a chunk of hair. Her attacker had loosened their grip just enough for Alex to gulp a breath of air. With renewed determination, Alex kicked her heel back and connected with her attacker's shin. The grip on her neck loosened even more, but the attacker didn't let go.

Alex finally was able to twist her body, punching, but her fists failed to connect with the attacker. Her heart pounded as she struggled to escape. Gasping for air, she spun around again, freeing herself from the death grip on her neck at last. Through her hazy vision, Alex glimpsed a familiar face, from the party. "Comare," she choked out.

The woman reached for her brooch, and without thinking, Alex tackled her, causing the Comare to stagger backward. Alex saw her attacker's expression flash to shock. Kibbles, with her doggy teeth bared, jumped at the woman, growling and barking fiercely. The Comare tripped over the small dog but regained her balance and ran off into the shadows made by the theater building, and scurried down the street. Alex collapsed on the bench, gasping for breath and shaking.

Alex was alive and had physically fought off her attacker. Kibbles barked her alarm call and then whined. Tears streaming down her face, Alex picked Kibbles up and hugged her tightly. "Shh baby, it's over. Shh. I'm okay. We're okay."

Alex wiped her face and waited a beat until her heart rate settled and she had her bearings, before dashing back to the house. She slammed the door behind her and slumped against the safety of the solid wood. As her adrenaline faded, Alex was overcome by disappointment that she'd let her guard down. *I almost paid the ultimate price for it.*

Kibbles still sounding her alarm call, Liam rushed into the sitting room, and Charlotte and Chirp bounded down the steps. All three converged on Alex at the same time. She was sitting on the couch taking deep breaths and trying to calm the dog.

Liam and Charlotte eyed her with concerned expressions. Charlotte bombarded her with questions. "What's wrong with Kibbles? Why'd you slam the door? What happened, Alex?"

Alex took measured breaths, trying to steady her nerves. "I was attacked in the courtyard," she said, her voice shaking.

Liam's and Charlotte's eyes widened in shock, and they immediately moved closer. Charlotte sat beside her and reached out for the trembling dog.

"I'll keep her, she's comforting me."

"Tell us what happened," Liam said.

"I took the dog out to pee," Alex explained, her voice still quivering. "And then out of nowhere, someone came up behind me and grabbed me. They put their hands around my neck and choked me from behind."

Liam gasped. "Are you hurt?" he asked, his eyes filled with concern.

Alex shook her head. "No, I fought her off."

"I'll get you a mug of tea, it will calm your nerves." Liam rushed out of the room.

"The attack was scary, but I'm calm. Now, I'm just mad," Alex said to Charlotte.

"Did you see who it was?" Charlotte asked, her voice tight with anger.

"The Comare!" Alex snarled and patted the dog until she stopped barking, and then stopped shaking.

Liam returned minutes later. "Here's some calming tea. I called Detective Bronco, also."

"What can he do? She slinked off down the street. I'm sure she's long gone by now."

"Still, we can review the footage from the security cameras," Liam replied.

"Thank you, I know you are trying to be helpful."

Liam nodded.

Charlotte paced in front of Alex who was still sitting on the couch with Kibbles. "She's pretty brazen to come here, crash the party and then attack you the next morning."

"She is certainly stepping up her game." Alex added fiercely, "She lost with Lilith."

"And she lost with the Italian couple on the cruise ship," Charlotte murmured.

"So what recourse does she have left but to take matters into her own hands," Liam added.

"But why does she want me dead?"

"She must realize at this point, you'll be taking over the Society of Six. So that makes you a threat to her," Charlotte replied.

Alex sipped the tea. It really was calming. "But why?" she asked. "What threat does the SOS pose against her?"

"I don't know—Yet," Liam replied. "But now we know for sure 'who' we're dealing with. We just need to figure out 'why.'"

There was a knock at the door, and Alex's heart leapt into her throat even though she knew it must be the detective, coming to take the report about the attack.

And I thought this anxiety of being attacked multiple times was finally passing.

Liam went to answer the door. Alex overheard his greeting. "Detective. Come in, she's in the sitting room."

Bronco followed Liam into the room.

"Detective Bronco," Alex greeted him but didn't stand up, though relief instantly flooded over her at his presence.

Detective Bronco sat in the armchair across from her, taking out his notepad and pen. "Are you okay? Do you want to tell me what happened?"

Alex took a deep breath and recounted the attack, telling him everything that had happened.

The detective nodded. "I suspect, when she couldn't overcome you physically, she was going to try to poison you with whatever was on, or in, her brooch." He sat back, a contemplative expression on his face. "I'll do everything I can, to find her—if she's still in town," he added. "But I'm sure she hightailed it out of here."

"I appreciate it."

"Liam, can we get together later to review the recordings from this morning?"

"Yes, of course."

"Alex, I'll stay around as long as you need me. In the meantime, I'd recommend you be careful and take precautions when you leave the house, in case she didn't leave town. Hopefully, she won't come back for a third attempt."

Liam and Charlotte sat on either side of Alex, offering her their silent support.

"I'll call for a few squad cars to patrol the area."

"Good." Alex nodded. "I've been on guard, after realizing the Comare was at the party last night." She paused. "But when I woke up this morning, I was distracted." She gave the detective a pleading glance before muttering, "By the birds."

18

HEART TO HEART

NERVOUSLY RUBBING HER SORE NECK, ALEX SAT ACROSS the table from Charlotte. Before them, lay an Italian spread, enough to feed the whole troupe. Alex had been procrastinating having this conversation for weeks—the words always stuck in her mind and never made it to her mouth. Kibbles was occupied, quietly licking herself under the table.

Alex inhaled a deep breath of the savory aroma of garlic and herbs that was wafting in the air.

"Charlotte," Alex started in a shaky voice as she served herself a small piece of lasagna from the casserole dish on the dining room table. "I've felt like an imposter for the last few months. I don't know if I'm telling you this because of the play, the actors, the detective, or what."

Charlotte stared back at Alex, with concern. "What do you mean?"

"I don't think I'm cut out for this. I've been pretending to be okay, when I'm really not. Pretending I know what I'm doing, but I'm struggling."

Charlotte reached for Alex's hand. "I'm sorry, I always

thought you had it all together. I wouldn't have known otherwise."

"Like I said, imposter." Alex circled her index finger in front of herself.

Charlotte made herself a plate. "What exactly are you faking?"

"That I know how to handle Nona's death, how to fill her shoes." Alex blew out a deep breath. "Investigate murders." She turned her head away. "Not get murdered, myself!"

Charlotte didn't speak. She blew on the fork full of steaming lasagna.

Alex used the pause in the conversation to appreciate a few bites of the delicious meal. "I feel like it's all been *reactive.* I keep having to react to all the situations I keep finding myself in. I can't seem to get ahead of it."

"Why didn't you tell me all this sooner? We could've worked it out together." Charlotte poured two generous glasses of wine.

"I didn't want you to think less of me, or think that I was weak."

Charlotte reached for Alex's hand again and squeezed it reassuringly. "You're not weak, Alex. You're one of the strongest people I know." She flashed a sympathetic look toward Alex and said, "I'm here for you, and we'll figure this out."

"Thank you for understanding, Charlotte," Alex replied, her voice barely above a whisper. She drank half the glass of wine, before devouring more of the pasta.

"I understand more than most. I've been muddling through life for years. Too many years."

"I've never said this out loud to anyone, but the guilt I feel is unbearable sometimes."

"What guilt?" Charlotte asked softly.

"About my parents for one—a foolish teenage argument I

replay over and over in my mind, and the last conversation I had with my dad before their accident. And, of course, the guilt about Nona. *You* know how I feel. I couldn't save her, and although I realize *she* was protecting *me,* from forces that were unknown to me, I still feel responsible."

"Alex—" Charlotte's eyes glazed over, and she lowered her head.

"I know. I know you feel that too."

Kibbles whined, interrupting the sad moment, and both women wiped their eyes dry.

A few minutes later, Charlotte interrupted the silence, "I think I might be in love."

Alex laughed, grateful for the change in conversation to something less heavy. "I've heard you say that a dozen times. At least."

"No, this time it's real. I know it."

Alex's heart skipped a beat at the heartfelt smile on her friends face. "With who?"

"Dave," Charlotte said, her eyes sparkling. "The handyman."

Alex couldn't believe it. Her best friend had fallen in love with someone she'd just met days ago. "That's amazing, Charlotte," she said in a supportive tone. "But what does that mean for you?"

"I'm staying in Mishap," Charlotte blurted with a nod. If it was possible for her smile to get any bigger, it spread across her face. "You don't want to live here, and someone needs to take care of the house and property. And the quilt studio." Her eyes sparkled.

"And Liam," Alex added.

"Exactly. So, I'll stay here and be the new keeper for the Society of Six. It's perfect for me. Besides, I've been couch surfing for way too long. I'm in my forties. I should be settled by now."

Alex's jaw dropped. *Charlotte's growing up, finally.*

"And it'll be okay if things don't work out with Dave," Charlotte said, and then hesitated. "But I know it will. This time it's different. He's not the typical bad boy that I usually go for. He's sweet and kind . . . and genuine . . . and handy." She winked.

"Charlotte, I don't know what to say. I'm thrilled for you. And of course you can stay here. You're right, it is perfect." Alex leaned forward in her chair. "I'm going to miss you terribly." Tears welled up in her eyes again, and she wiped them with her napkin. "Look at us, getting all emotional!"

"I know, Alex," Charlotte said, taking Alex's hand. "But we'll still talk all the time, and I'll keep you up to date on all things *Mishap*."

Alex nodded; Charlotte was right about both, Dave and staying in Georgia—Alex could see the difference in Charlotte, the way she had blossomed in the short time they'd been here. "I really am happy for you, Charlotte."

"Thank you, Alex. I'm excited for this new adventure."

Alex took a deep breath. "While we're at it, I've made a few life-changing decisions of my own, Charlotte."

"Ooh, juicy. Do tell!"

"I've been doing a lot of thinking while we've been here." Alex sipped her cocoa, and Charlotte refilled her water glass, from the pitcher on the table. Alex continued, "About my own future. I've decided I'm going to retire."

"Retire? From what? You're in your forties!" Charlotte leaned back in her chair. "I thought you basically retired when you left New York. You haven't practiced law since you've been back to Spruce Street."

Alex chuckled a nervous laugh. "Retire from work, from everything. I want to take a break and enjoy my life." Alex paused. "With Hawk. I'm going to ask him to move to Madras with me." Her face flushed.

Charlotte's eyes widened, and she smiled. "Wow, that's bold."

"I know. I'm nervous, but I think it's the right decision."

"You have nothing to be nervous about. He is crazy about you, Alex."

"You think so?"

"Yes, of course. It's a no-brainer." Charlotte laughed obnoxiously.

Alex beamed.

Charlotte looked concerned. "Wait, if I'm staying here and you're running off to an exotic island . . ."

"I wouldn't call it exotic, maybe dilapidated."

"Ha, ha. Who's going to maintain your house, and support Spruce Street?"

"Well, I've given that some thought also. Joey can move into number 1. He's graduating school soon. And Pepper can keep an eye on Spruce Street. With Betty's help, of course."

"Woof." Alex eyed Kibbles lounging on the floor, by her feet.

"And Nona's help, from beyond the grave," Charlotte whispered.

Alex patted Kibbles, who was suddenly alert and standing on her hind legs, leaning against Alex's chair, begging to be picked up. "A wedding is in their future, and what better gift?"

"Than handing over the reins to the next generation? That's a nice gift from you, but you better make sure it's something Pepper and Joey actually want first. You said yourself, you felt ill equipped when all this was thrown in your lap, and at twice their age." Charlotte clapped, and Chirp ran to her side of the table. She moved her hands, and the cat jumped into her lap.

"You really have taken to this place." Alex chuckled. "I thought you hated cats?"

"Chirp, chirp, chirp," the tomcat let out an alarm.

"Shh." Charlotte covered the cat's ears and smiled. "Big changes for all of us," Charlotte said absentmindedly while stroking the cat's back. "When are you planning on making the move?"

"Not for some time still. We have the Father's Day picnic, then I'm going to visit Madras to make a plan. I'm thinking midsummer. Joey will be done with his classes by then."

"Maybe a fall wedding for the young love birds?" Charlotte waggled her eyebrows.

"I'm not going to pressure Joey. There's no rush on that front. He and Pepper are still so young," Alex replied.

"I'll come back to help, and for a wedding, of course!"

"You are welcome to bring Dave to Spruce Street or Madras anytime. Nothing will change between *us*." Alex flashed her a reassuring smile, more for herself than for Charlotte's benefit.

"Absolutely! Maybe an island wedding?" Charlotte teased. The jumbo cat jumped off her lap and landed on the floor with a thud. "Had enough, buddy?"

"Let's not get too far ahead of ourselves, now."

"A murder mystery wedding? Could be fun, just saying." Charlotte shrugged.

"With my luck, that's exactly what it would be!" Alex replied, then yawned.

"I'm tired too." Charlotte slipped off her chair. "Call it a night?"

"As long as you don't disappear overnight to start your new life with Dave!" Alex teased.

"Very funny." Charlotte smiled, and they both headed up to bed—Kibbles and Chirp following.

19

HE'S NO FOOL

ALEX, CHARLOTTE AND LIAM SAT AT BREAKFAST IN THE lavish dining room when suddenly a gust of cool air flooded the room, and a door slammed. Alex stiffened, still worried about the Comare returning.

"Just me!" Detective Bronco called, and Alex leaned back in her chair and breathed a sigh of relief.

"In here," Liam called out.

Entering the dining room, Bronco paused to lean against the door frame. Dressed in a designer suit, he looked ten years younger than he had the day before. And was surprisingly no longer balding.

"Wow, what a difference!" Charlotte exclaimed. "Alex told me about your charade, but I had no idea the extent of it."

Bronco's expression brightened as Charlotte gave him the once-over.

Gone were the balding wig and wrinkled forehead and the stomach pouch. Before them stood a silver fox in a slim linen Bahama suit. The worn, beat-up fedora was replaced with a sharp Panama hat.

Alex flushed. *Hubba, hubba.*

What is it with fine men, who are just my type, distracting me everywhere I go? It's been too long!

"Are you on duty, Aames?" Liam asked.

"No, I just wanted to follow up with you all, before Alex and Charlotte left."

Charlotte grinned. "Oh, I'm staying. This place is too awesome to leave!"

Liam pointed. "Pull up a chair and enjoy a mimosa."

Detective Aames Bronco tipped his hat to the women before taking it off and placing it on an empty chair. He feathered his full head of salt-and-pepper hair back into place with his hand.

"So you were in on it too?" Alex asked Liam.

"I'm sorry if it feels like a deception."

"No, all is well. We got the killer. Well, one of them, anyway."

Charlotte raised her glass to Aames. "You *acted* like a fool?" Charlotte asked incredulously. "I was really beginning to hate you."

Aames nodded. "Yes, I did act foolish. But sometimes you have to think outside the box to solve a case. And in this instance, the act of *acting* worked perfectly, given the setting." He winked at Charlotte, who didn't bat an eye. "The theatrics were starting to get to me as well," he admitted. "It was hard to stay in character. I guess I'm not cut out to be a full-time actor." He flashed a charming smile, but Charlotte still didn't bother with him. "Well, I hope you decided against hate?"

"Sure, sure," Charlotte murmured, distracted by her phone. "Why did you pretend to choke? Even I knew that was a charade."

"Taking the measure of the suspects. Harrison at least acted like he was trying to save me, but Emmie stood by to let me choke to death."

"Oh, right, oh-kay" Charlotte murmured with her head down, still concentrating on her phone. "Why the ruse with arresting Emmie?"

"To catch the real murderer, of course." Bronco winked but Charlotte was oblivious to it.

Alex smiled. "Well, I have to hand it to you. You certainly have a way of getting the job done."

"Thanks, Alex. I'll take that as a compliment."

Charlotte finally looked up from her phone. "Did you see the headlines?" She turned her phone around to show everyone and said, "*Hotshot Detective Single-Handedly Catches Murderous Actor.*"

Everyone leaned in.

"Pff, figures," Charlotte added a moment later.

A cocky expression lit up Detective Bronco's face.

Alex poured maple syrup and scooped slices of peaches onto her pancakes. "Breakfast? There's plenty. Make yourself a plate." *If you're not too busy preening like a peacock.*

She nodded to the buffet, where steaming chafing dishes of food lined the credenza along the length of the wall.

"It's all locally sourced," Liam commented.

"So good," Charlotte said in a lyrical voice. "Try the peach tartlets."

Detective Bronco took off his khaki blazer and draped it over the back of the chair. "I'll have you know, I have a reputation for being one of the finest detectives in the country," he said, and then unbuttoned and rolled up his sleeves.

You can say that again!

"So you knew everything that was going on?" Charlotte asked. Alex hid a smile. *Charlotte's attention toward the detective likely has to do with the fact that she's already finished her third mimosa. And now she's beckoning for a fourth.*

"No, I had it wrong at first also. I was convinced it was Emmie."

Alex chimed in, "Right. The whole disgruntled, under-appreciated assistant spiel."

"Clever name for a country girl," Charlotte quipped and let out a soft burp. "Excuse me!" Charlotte's face flushed red from her embarrassment, and Alex smelled the chives from the scrambled eggs.

The detective casually ignored her outburst, and Alex changed the subject. "How did you know about the secret exit?"

He loaded his plate with fluffy eggs and then squirted ketchup all over them.

"Yuck," Charlotte whispered, and Alex swatted in her direction playfully. He started a second plate, adding bacon, sausage and ham before turning back to the table and setting his plates down.

Where's he gonna put all that food?

Answering Alex's earlier question, Bronco said, "Where do you think I studied for the *Man From La Mancha* play?"

He barely managed a bite before Charlotte asked, "Here?" She buttered a piece of toast and slathered it with peach jam.

He responded while cutting his ham steak, "Yes, some years ago."

While Alex admired the detective's physique and out of the box crime solving technique, Charlotte plastered a fake smile on her face, and everyone continued eating.

"I'm going to miss these breakfasts when I leave, Liam," Alex said.

Kibbles confirmed. "Woof!"

Charlotte not so inconspicuously treated the pup to a whole slice of bacon under the table.

"I saw that," Alex said in a low voice, and Charlotte shrugged.

The detective swallowed. "That reminds me, I got a plate number for the car driven by the woman who tried to kill you. Captured it on a security camera we've had down the street."

"Comare?" Alex uttered before gulping down her mimosa.

"I don't follow? Is she your godmother, Alex?"

"No. She's the Godmother of the Mafia in New York." Charlotte answered and then chuckled. "Didn't you know?"

"Things certainly are entertaining around here," the detective said, and poured himself a drink.

Alex raised her eyebrows. "That's an understatement." She pushed her glass toward him and nodded for him to fill hers as well.

He obliged, carefully filling her goblet without spilling a drop. "So, what's next for you, Alex?"

Is he flirting with me? No, stop, Alex.

"I'm headed back to Massachusetts. I suspect Hawk and I will make significant progress in our investigation, now that we have some leads, thanks to Liam."

Aames flashed her a questioning look.

"Hawk is a local PI who's been on the case with me since I lived and worked in New York."

"I'd like to meet this investigator of yours."

Of mine. Alex swooned. Then she pulled herself together. "I'm sure that could be arranged."

Detective Bronco looked away and asked, "And you're staying with us here in Mishap, Charlotte?"

"Yup, me and Dave, Dave and I, we . . . we are an item now." She giggled.

"You're shut off," Alex said and put her hand over Charlotte's cup.

"Excellent," Aames said, then whispered to Alex, "Who's Dave?" and winked.

After breakfast, the whole gang met at the theater and Liam called the cast in to explain all that had transpired over New Year's, to alert them about Charlotte, and to give Alex and Kibbles a chance to say goodbye.

"Thank you for coming in today. I have some news to share with you all. I am happy to say, Charlotte will be staying on with us. She will be my second in charge, so whatever you need from me, you will be able to go to her for, in time."

"Except for hemming, buttons, zippers or other costume sewing." Charlotte counted off on her fingers the things she wasn't willing to do. "Or coffee."

Alex laughed.

"And Alex and Kibbles are leaving."

A volley of "Awes" came from the crowd as Kibbles jumped around on her hind legs.

Looks like the dog ended up being the star of the show.

"And as you may know, Emmie was arrested for Roy's murder but has been released. She is welcome to come back when she is ready. And the detective has made his apologies."

Several actors groaned, and Charlotte whispered, "Sounds like they were happy to be rid of her."

Charlotte will fit right into this soap opera. Days of Mishap.

"The same evidence that allowed us to release Emmie led us to find the air-tight solution and Harrison has rightfully been charged with Roy's murder."

But Alex knew that arresting Emmie was just another ruse to get the real killer to relax and reveal themselves.

Suzie slouched into one of the theater seats.

Charlotte whispered, "I think she had a thing for Harrison."

"Thanks for the play-by-play," Alex replied in a low voice. "Shh."

"I did have a thing for him, but I thought he was with Jojo," Suzie commented.

Alex pressed her lips together. *I guess Charlotte wasn't quiet, enough.*

"I think we just stumbled on our motive. Did Jojo tell us she was with Roy?" Charlotte asked.

"No, she must have lied," Alex replied.

All eyes turned toward Jojo.

Detective Bronco appeared by Liam's side. "That's correct, Jojo lied. But Harrison did admit to killing Roy in a fit of jealousy."

"I didn't lie, Roy and I weren't in a relationship yet," Jojo protested. "And I broke it off with Harrison when I found out Roy was smitten with me."

Ignoring Jojo, the detective continued, "Harrison admitted that he did something he now regrets. Unfortunately for Roy, it's much too late." Detective Bronco shook his head sadly. "He followed Roy and Jojo, and when they snuck around after breakfast, he laid in wait for Roy to be by himself. He lured Roy with a personal mending project." The detective faced Alex and Charlotte. "It seems your grandmother, Nona, taught Roy well, in the stitching department."

"Thank you, Detective. Fine work." Liam shook hands with him before turning back to the group. "Now, we've had some trouble on another matter. A woman we'll refer to for now as Comare. I'll provide you with a description and a sketch later, and you can all keep an eye out for her. I believe the danger has passed for the moment, but we must stick together and be vigilant. If you see anything unusual, or suspect anything nefarious is happening, let us know, right away."

As they listened to Liam's news, the actors exchanged whispers and furtive glances amongst each other.

It's clear something is going on—does the group know more than Liam thinks they do? Has the secret of the Society of Six come out?

Alex listened to the chatter from the actors who were gathered by the soundboard toward the back of the dimly lit theater.

"About that..." Dave raised his hand. "We know all about the secret society, Liam, so there's really no need to be hush-hush." Dave sat and kicked his legs up onto the equipment stand, and Liam eyed him. Dave cleared his throat and removed his feet.

"Liam *tries* to hide it," Wallace said.

As the murmurs and conversations continued, it became clear that each person on staff had some knowledge about the SOS.

Liam face flushed.

Suzie let him off the hook. "*I* heard it from my Uncle Aames," Suzie said.

Alex and Charlotte exchanged looks, and Alex mouthed, "I didn't know he knew."

"I found out from Roy. He stumbled upon the secret lair one day while looking for supplies," Norman told the group.

"I overheard Nona discussing it during her last visit. It's kind of creepy, though, isn't it?" Jojo said, shivering a little. "I mean, who knows what kind of stuff we're dealing with."

Wallace leaned in, his eyes gleaming. "Solving murders, apparently! Duh."

"Which is no different than what we already do in our spare time," Norman added matter-of-factly.

"So they all think they're amateur sleuths." Charlotte guffawed. "Didn't do much good for Roy."

"Charlotte!" Alex chided her friend.

Kibbles barked in alarm, and Alex bent to pick her up.

"Hey, I'm in charge now," Charlotte replied with a mock evil look on her face.

"Woof!"

"Yeah, well, don't let it go to your head," Alex said, and ruffled the fur on Kibbles's head.

20

WHAT NEXT?

THE FIRE WAS BLAZING, ITS LIGHT FLICKERING OFF THE mirrors hanging around the oversized sitting room. A room the size of two of Alex's rooms back at number 1 Spruce Street.

Liam held Alex's hands as he said, "I'm sad to see you leave. It's been a real pleasure meeting you and having you here."

Alex hugged him. "I hate to leave, but I must get back. There's always stitching concerns to be tended to," Alex said. He kissed her on the cheek and let her go.

"Liam, before I go, I need to know about this play. I expected it to be about quilting."

"Your guess is as good as mine. I left that up to Suzie, and Nona—she was the Quibah after all."

Alex chuckled and Liam leaned in to whisper in her ear, "Suzie's a special girl, keen like her uncle... And Nona indulged her fancy."

I'm not even sure what that means?

Alex sighed. "Okay, we'll leave it at that."

He slipped his hand into the pocket of his knit cardigan, pulled something out and then placed a key in her hand. "You take this. Now you have four of the six."

"And you have no idea what they belong to?"

He shook his head and backed away. "I have a few more things for you."

Liam left the room, and Charlotte shrugged and shook her head.

Not a minute passed before he came back with a large basket.

"What is all this?" Alex asked, and sat on the edge of the settee. Liam set the picnic basket next to her.

Alex poked through the basket. Inside she found a stack of journals bound together with a leather tie. "What are these?"

"I hope you will find more answers in those. The top two were Nona's personal journals, and the bottom two were passed down through the Society. I don't have the cipher for those, but I enclosed the LIAM cipher in Nona's."

Alex rubbed her fingers over the bound journals, imagining Nona's thoughts. She flipped the bundle over and traced the embossed symbol for the SOS. Her breath hitched before she responded. "Thank you!"

Underneath the journals lay a couple of sandwiches, bottles of water and a personal charcuterie board, as well as peanut butter snacks for Kibbles. Alex glanced up at Liam. Her eyes pricked, and she held the tears back. "Thank you. You are amazing. I just can't thank you enough for everything!"

"No need. Please do not hesitate to contact me with any questions you may have. I am at your disposal."

"Don't say it like that, it's kinda grim."

"I'm serious, and there's a phone in the care package as well. My personal number is already programmed in."

"And mine," Charlotte chimed in, and waved a small flip phone at Alex, then slipped it into her pocket.

Kibbles whined.

"What, you want a phone too? You don't even have thumbs." Charlotte picked up the dog and squeezed her.

"Wooof, wooof," Kibbles protested.

"One more thing, Alex."

Liam went to the roll-top desk in the far corner of the sitting room and pulled out a small wooden box that fit in the palm of his hand. "Here. I think the contents will help you clear your family of Eleanor's murder."

"What is it?"

"Don't trouble yourself with it now. Just wait until you get home. It's been a long week. Besides, I've had it hanging around for a long while...And it won't spoil."

Alex smiled appreciatively at her new friend and her old friend. The smile in her heart reached down to her toes.

Liam handed her his handkerchief, and she caught an errant tear with it. "I love you both."

"Come on, you're going to make me cry too!" Charlotte crossed the room and gave Alex a huge hug.

"Well, I better get to packing or I'll never get out of here."

After a quick lunch, Alex packed the rest of her things. *It's much later than I anticipated. I wanted to be on the road this morning.*

Kibbles barked twice as if she knew what Alex was thinking.

"You're anxious to get home to Hawk too, aren't you?"

"Woooooof!" She let out a long approving bark.

"As much as I want to get home, I am sad to leave." Alex tucked her toiletry bag into her pack and zipped it up.

Charlotte poked her head in. "I think I'll take this room.

The light is better, and the morning sun doesn't come in so early."

"You gonna jump in my grave that fast?" Alex ribbed her, and set her bag on the floor.

"Funny." Charlotte came all the way into the room, and Kibbles leapt into her arms as soon as she reached the bed. "Yes, I will miss you too, you little troublemaker."

"Woof, woof."

"Noooo, not you. You're not a troublemaker," Charlotte said sarcastically, laughed and then kissed the dog, on her head.

The cat slinked in and wrapped his tail around Alex's leg. "Chirrrp."

"Well, sir, I will miss you." Alex petted the cat down the length of his back and shook off a handful of ginger cat hair.

"I'm sad to be leaving without you." Alex pouted and reached out to hug Charlotte. They squeezed Kibbles between them.

"Me too. Maybe I'll come back for the Father's Day picnic. Maybe by then we'll have new paw-in-laws." Charlotte waggled her eyebrows.

"Whose, yours or mine?" Alex asked. "No, don't answer, let's leave it at that."

"Are you sure you're okay to make the trip back by yourself?"

"Woof." Kibbles squirmed out of Charlotte's arms, and Alex reached out for her.

"I won't be alone, I have my girl."

"Woof."

"Take care of Liam. He's a peach!"

"I will, don't worry. I've got this," Charlotte replied, and sat on the bed. "This mattress is nicer too."

Alex shook her head. "I'm almost ready."

Kibbles and Chirp spent the next ten minutes chasing each other through the main house. Alex caught sight of them skidding by several times as she packed the car.

"Come, Kibbles, it's time to go." Kibbles bounded down the steps, calling out her three-bark alarm call, with Chirp caterwauling behind her.

"You two will meet again, I'm sure," Alex reassured the pup.

"Woof," Kibbles confirmed.

Chirp agreed with his signature, "Chirp."

Who knows what this new year will bring?

Liam followed them out, Chirp slinking around them and jumping onto the hood of Alex's SUV.

"They'll be the best of friends. Since they both come from royal bloodlines," Liam noted.

"Royal pain in the a—" Alex joked.

Both animals rebuked that notion. "Chirp, chirp!" "Woof, woof."

She put Kibbles into her seat, and the pooch wriggled out of it.

"I'm blaming this on your cat, Liam. I'm never going to get her to stay in that seat, now that she's a master escape artist!"

Alex scooched the dog over to the passenger side and lunged into the car, then shut the door and pressed the window control button.

The window lowered, and cool Georgia air flooded in. Alex surveyed the house, courtyard and theater, taking one last mental picture. She grinned at the purple pansies and heart their heart-shaped leaves. *I can't believe we thought Liam's house was haunted.*

"Thank you for everything, Liam. I appreciate all you've done for us this past week. Including taking in Charlotte."

"It's my pleasure. We're going to get a lot of work done."

Alex eyed him speculatively and put the car in gear, then pulled around in the opposite direction so she could drive past the theater and see the mural. She waved to Liam, Chirp, and Charlotte as she passed by. Kibbles barked in protest.

"Should I have left you behind to stay with the Society?"

"Woof, woof, woof." Kibbles howled her alarm.

"I know, I couldn't. It would break my heart." Kibbles climbed up her arm and perched on her shoulder before licking her up the nose.

"Gross, Kibbles. Stop, I'm driving."

She pulled over at the end of the block. "Let's get a look at Nona, shall we?"

She stepped out of the car and marveled at the two-story mural of Gretta Galia, aka Nona, hand-stitching huge hexagons into one of her signature quilts. "It's my graduation quilt, Kibbles!"

Kibbles woofed once, and Alex beamed up at the mural with pride.

EPILOGUE

JANUARY 2ND

NEARLY HOME FROM MISHAP, GEORGIA, ALEX BRISTLED, pondering the events of the past week. She glanced up into the rearview mirror of her luxury SUV, still paranoid that someone, maybe even the Comare, might be following her.

"Well, Kibbles, let's hope there's no more drama between now and Father's Day. We have the annual picnic and hot-dog-eating contest coming up in a few months."

Kibbles licked her own lips and barked once in approval. Hot dogs were one of the mutt's guilty pleasures.

That'll give me enough time to research the new clues that Liam provided.

Alex flexed her shoulder. It had gone numb from having a ten-pound furball perched on it for the last two hours. She scratched the pooch on the head, and Kibbles returned the love by licking Alex's cheek.

"Thank you!" she replied, wiping her face. "Let's pull off to the rest area for a pit stop. Just three more hours until we get home to Massachusetts!"

"Woof."

I wonder if Hawk will surprise us and be there when we get home?

Flicking her blinker on, she pulled into the travel stop and checked the mirrors again before parking. She turned off the ignition, pried the dog off her shoulder, and clipped a leash onto Kibbles. She reached for the door handle, and her phone pinged with an incoming text.

HAWK:

Almost home?

ALEX:

Couple more hours.

Stopping for relief right now.

HAWK:

Okay. I'll meet you there. Be safe!

Alex smiled and led Kibbles to the pet area. *We'll see each other soon. Now, I'm sure of it.*

Read the next book in the series, Stitching Concerns, today!

Leave a review!

Thank you for reading my book!
I appreciate your feedback and love to hear about how you enjoyed it!

Please leave a positive review letting me know what you thought.

BONUS: BETWEEN THREADING TROUBLE AND PAW-IN-LAW

AUGUST

After the misadventure during the Father's Day picnic, a flood of excitement washed over Alex. Summer was waning in New England as she planned a much needed getaway to her island, Madras, with Hawk.

ALEX:

I'll meet you there. I'm flying this time.

HAWK:

Don't want to risk another quilting calamity?

ALEX:

Funny, and no, I don't!

HAWK:

Whatever it takes to steal you away.

ALEX:

I'm all yours, no thievery needed.

HAWK:

But it might be fun?

ALEX:

Just fun in the sun!

She set her phone on the bed. "It's time for me to pack now, Kibbles," Alex said to the napping dog curled up in a ball. "I can't put it off any longer."

Celia Moore—the local travel agent in Salem, Massachusetts—had made the final arrangements for Alex's flight, and Hawk was booked on the cruise ship *Tranquility*, leaving the week before Alex. With any luck, nothing would go wrong and they'd both arrive on the same day.

"Woof, woof," Kibbles protested.

"I'm sorry. It'll only be a week apart, and then Pepper and Joey will bring you to the island when they come."

"Woof, woof."

"You'll have fun with Pepper! I'm sure she'll spoil you rotten."

Kibbles jumped off the bed and ran in circles, doing zoomies on the braided rug, showing her approval of being spoiled by her favorite friend and pet chef, Pepper Grace.

"We'll be busy with the repairs on the school and the house. You stay here and have fun. I'm going to get everything ready for you, and we'll spend the rest of the year with our toes in the sand!"

Kibbles said no with a "Woof, woof!"

"Okay, our toes *and paws* in the sand."

Kibbles spun around two more times before plopping on Alex's toes and barking.

"Yes, those toes. But I need them to pack. So, scooch!"

A QUILTING COZY MYSTERY

STITCHING CONCERNS

KATHRYN MYKEL

STITCHING CONCERNS BLURB

Stitching concerns and a thread of truth. Can Alex take back control of her life, and put her embroidered past behind her before she's bound?

Alex Bailey's mind is layered with ambivalence. A trip to Madras Island is exactly what this quilter has ordered. A kidnapping thwarts her travel and romantic rendezvous with Hawk. Just when she thinks she's solved the mystery, a murder threatens to derail her once again. Can she arrange the details of the tangled threads before she's stitching in a ditch?

As Alex uncovers a patchwork of secrets, will her quest for the truth also unravel everything she's ever known?

Stitching Concerns is the dramatic fifth book in a series of Quilting Cozy Mysteries. This book will keep you hooked until the very last stitch. If you like gripping whodunits, then you'll love Kathryn Mykel's whipstitched tale.

Buy Stitching Concerns to unknot a methodical crime today!

STITCHING CONCERNS: CHAPTER 1

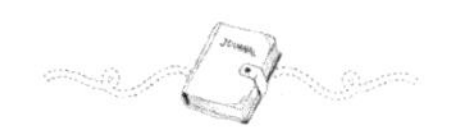

ALEX

In the dim glow of a Tiffany lamp, Alex's heart was burdened by nostalgia and curiosity. She clutched her deceased, adoptive grandmother's journal. Still longing for her own parents after the Father's Day festivities, Alex sprawled out on the sofa and began reading about Nona's adventures.

Alex had taken the diary from Nona's bureau on Madras Island during her stop there, on the quilting calamity cruise. All the excitement leading up to her trip to Mishap, Georgia, had kept her from reading it until now.

A page was marked by one of Nona's hexagon fabric pieces and Alex began reading there. The entry from 2002, twenty years earlier, was scrawled in Nona's handwriting:

Darkness still blanketed our quiet, wholesome

Spruce Street neighborhood as we pulled up in front of number 9. When I stepped out of the car, I instantly filled my lungs with the fresh pine scent of the adjacent forest—it calmed me, but not for long. Liam was quick to join me with a proffered hand.

He's a fool—I'm sixty-five, not dead, Journal. I can carry my own bags.

The flight from Sudbury was turbulent, both physically and mentally, as Liam and I devised our plan for how to explain my sudden departure from Canadian soil to my traveling companion, Pauline Riddell, whom I'd just left in the lurch mid-vacation. And more importantly, how we were going to handle meeting the head of the New York City Mafia, Kaitlyn Romano, later today.

My friend Pauline is a shrewd sleuth, Journal, she won't rest, given she was shown a page full of obviously trumped-up charges by the Canadian detectives.

My choices are simple: tell her the truth about the SOS—Society of Six; or risk her friendship, and subsequently her vacationing companionship, with lies, or worse, my permanent absence.

After making the case to Liam, we both agreed Pauline could be trusted with the SOS information and should be told the truth. I would hate to lose *my friend, especially when things are just starting to get exciting.*

Alex flipped the page. *Well, that sort of explains why she was silenced in Sudbury.* Kibbles stirred, her soft snoring interrupted by something imperceptible to Alex's human senses.

Part of the 'truth' is that the society has far-reaching capabilities. This is due to the fact that it originated in the United Kingdom, migrated to Canada, and then finally made its home base in the United States–New York to be exact! Its capabilities include making people disappear...both for the good–my dear friend Rebecca, who must remain in hiding if she ever wants to live a normal life... and for the bad–the death of Eleanor Romano, which sadly Liam and I must confront later this very day.

Alex shuddered and ran her finger over the words 'death of Eleanor Romano.'

Read the next book in the series, Stitching Concerns, today!

ADDITIONAL BOOKS

Award-winning author of the best-selling quilting cozy mystery series:

Sewing Suspicion - 2021 Indie Cozy Mystery Book of The Year Quilting Calamity - 2022 Indie Cozy Mystery Book of The Year

Inspired by the laugh-out-loud and fanciful aspects of cozies, Kathryn aims to write lighthearted, humorous mysteries that play on her passion for the craft of quilting. She's an avid quilter, born and raised in a small New England town.

www.authorkathrynmykel.com

Quilting Cozy Mystery Series:

Sewing Suspicion (Book 1)
Quilting Calamity (Book 2)

Pressing Matters (Book 3)
Mutterly Mistaken
(Holiday Pet Sleuths Series) (Book 3.5)
Threading Trouble (Book 4)
Paw-in-Law
(Holiday Pet Sleuths Series) (Book 4.5)
Stitching Concerns (Book 5)
Purrfect Perpetrator
(Holiday Pet Sleuths Series) (Book 5.5)
Mending Mischief (Book 6)
Doggone Disaster
(Holiday Pet Sleuths Series) (Book 6.5)
Patchwork Perils (Book 7)
Seaming Uncertainty (Book 8)

~ Coming Soon ~

Beach Brawl (the book inside the books)
Whipstitching Worries (Book 9)
Needling Nemesis (Book 10)

Book Set 1
Includes Books (1-3):
Sewing Suspicion, Quilting Calamity & Pressing Matters
Book Set 2
Includes Books (1-5):
Sewing Suspicion, Quilting Calamity, Pressing Matters,
Threading Trouble & Stitching Concerns

<u>Stand-alone Books:</u>

I Pittie the Yule (Christmas Novella)

Dead End (Halloween Novella)
Fine Points Are Sketchy (Quilting Cozy Mystery)
A Load of Trouble

Cozy Mysteries by Kathryn Mykel & P.C. James:
Senior Sassy Sleuths Series
(Short Stories, Shared Main Characters)
Senior Sassy Sleuths
Senior Sassy Sleuths Return
Senior Sassy Sleuths on the Trail

Anthology Series
(Short stories by multiple authors)
A Cauldron of Deceptions
A Campsite of Culprits
A Vacation of Mischief
An Aquarium of Deceit
A Bookworm of A Suspect
A Festival of Forensics
A Haunting of Revenge
A Hiss-teria of Killers
A Hobby in Foul Play

1950s Cozy Mysteries by
Kathryn Mykel & P.C. James:
Duchess of Snodsbury Mysteries
Royally Dispatched, Royally Whacked, Royally Snuffed

Sweet & wholesome romance by Kathryn LeBlanc:

Quinn (Runaway Brides of the West Series)
Christmas Star Cottage (Holiday Cottage Series)
Sugar Cookie Inn (Christmas at the Inn Series)
Clara's Crusade (Suffrage Spinster Series)

Mail-Order Papa Series

A Banker for Bethany
A Carpenter for Catherine
A Lumberjack for Lorena

Honorable Husbands Series

Mail-Order Carpenter
Mail-Order Thief

Be the first to receive exclusive information about the Heatherton Series here:
https://authorkathrynmykel.myflodesk.com/readernewslettersignup

A crafty new series from award-winning author Kathryn Mykel stitches levity and suspense together with the charm of a fictitious small town on the coast of Maine, in this page-turning cozy mystery.

Website
www.authorkathrynmykel.com/heatherton

Raining Quilts and Dogs: A Quilting Cozy Mystery

Will the roof cave in on Elizabeth's new endeavor, or will she catch the murderer before she's basted?

Interior designer, Elizabeth Purdy has a notion to restore Saint Christina's Nunnery into a quilting retreat center but torrential downpours threaten to destroy the historic landmark before she even begins. When Elizabeth finds Heatherton's favorite neighbor and retired private investigator, Mr. Jenkins, murdered, face down in a puddle, she realizes that Mother Nature isn't the only villain on the loose.

With the deed and keys to the old monastery in hand, Elizabeth is in a race against time to pin down the culprit before tensions rise like the flood waters in this quiet, oceanside town. The quilters just wanna quilt, the neighborhood pets are barking Maine-iacs, and the town is completely cut off from their emergency services.

Raining Quilts and Dogs is the gripping first book in this new Quilting Cozy Mystery series. Stitched with suspicion, calamity, and threads of doubt, it will leave you needling for the next book.

Support Raining Quilts and Dogs to uncover an unexpected crime today!

https://www.kickstarter.com/projects/authorkathrynmykel/raining-quilts-and-dogs

Made in the USA
Middletown, DE
03 November 2024

63366184R00106